All Things Violent

This edition first published 2017 by Fahrenheit Press

10 9 8 7 6 5 4 3 2 1

www.Fahrenheit-Press.com

F 4 E

All Things Violent

By

Nikki Dolson

Fahrenheit Press

For Lee, who pushed me, and for Shane and Edmond, who cheered me on. I would be lost without y'all.

Evelyn Bright was gone. Only the faint scent of vanilla remained to prove she'd been there at all. I smelled it before when I searched her house. The scent clung to her clothes, lingering in the master bedroom and bathroom, fainter in the other rooms. I smelled vanilla again when Frank and I caught up with her husband and his mistress. In the car they were driving, it was slowly overwhelmed by the mistress's own flowery scent—a mixture of hairspray and cheap perfume.

Behind me the motel desk clerk exhaled loudly, shifting her weight from foot to foot, her nylon windbreaker rustling. In front of me there was an empty bed next to an equally empty dresser and closet, all this emptiness added up to a terribly empty room. Terrible because I was supposed to have found her here. Frank was gonna be pissed.

"Lady, are we done?" said Marie, my escort for the morning. The motel was near Tahoe and Marie was understandably irritated with me. I'd asked her to come outside in the drizzling rain an hour before the sunrise and take me to Evelyn Bright's room. I guess I was hoping the clerk got the room number wrong. That Evelyn was still there, waiting for her boyfriend to show.

"Show me the other rooms." I'd asked.

All were empty but two.

"Off-season for the tourist folk," she said back when she was still happy with me and the promise of money had put a bounce in her step.

I convinced her to let me knock on the two occupied rooms. In one room, a curly-haired business man, sleep still creasing his face. In the other, an older woman with deep bruises under her eyes and the stink of alcohol on her breath glared at me then demanded I went away.

We circled back to where we began; I insisted she open Evelyn's room again. I knew this was the right room. This was where Evelyn Bright was supposed to be sleeping. Only she wasn't here, her blue Chevy was not in the parking lot and the desk clerk hadn't seen her leave.

I handed the desk clerk the fifty I promised along with a business card with Pritchard Investigations embossed on one side and my cell phone number written on the back.

"If she comes back…" I said.

"Sure, sure," she said. But she wouldn't call. My card would end up in the day's garbage, which was fine. The card was a prop. Pritchard Investigations was a real business with a couple of PIs working out of the office, but I wasn't one of them. My skill set skewed a little differently.

I watched Marie walk away, the fifty already safe and warm and dry in her pocket, my card balled up in her fist. She was mannered enough not to throw it away in front of me. I got in my car and leaned my head against the steering wheel, pulled my cell phone from my pocket and hit redial.

Frank answered.

I explained.

"We should have gotten her last night," he said.

"I know, but you were too tired to drive and I can't drive two cars now can I?" I started the car, pulled out of the motel's parking lot and onto the highway. An eighteen-wheeler flew past, blowing its horn, shaking the car and me.

Two days ago, Frank decided he couldn't handle driving with me anymore. I guess I got too chatty. We spent an hour cruising malls until he found the Jetta I was driving now. He spent the rest of the trip calling me repeatedly, taunting—"Come on, Cupcake. Keep up," while he drove ninety miles an hour and I maintained the posted speed limit. I finally shut my cell phone off. Maybe if we hadn't stopped for his car-stealing venture we wouldn't have missed Evelyn.

The plausible excuses kept coming. Deflect, deflect, deflect the blame. "It's not my fault she's not where the guy said she'd be," I said.

The guy, Travis—tired of running errands for our clients and sweet on Mrs. Evelyn Bright— had been our only lead. We'd caught him laying low in a motel in Arizona. After Frank beat him until he told us everything—Bright had called him declaring her love and hoping he would meet her so they could disappear together—we dropped him off with our clients, business men in their sixties who dealt in everything, according to Frank: prostitution, drugs, gambling. You name it; they were scoring a piece of it from somewhere.

Our clients were anxious to have someone take the blame for a few million disappearing. The screams I heard as we were leaving their place, a big house in Palm Springs, were horror movie quality—high-pitched and heartfelt. It's funny, but I thought Frank felt bad about leaving him to his fate. However, with Frank, it's business before conscience.

I switched the phone to my other ear and heard Frank groan, the bed creaking under his weight. He was a big man, six four and weighed in at a respectable two fifty. I pictured him nice and warm in his motel room, the twin of mine, sitting on the edge of the uncomfortable bed, and I wondered what he slept in. Boxers? In the buff? A vision of Frank's muscled bulk in nothing but a sheet skittered past, chased away by the memory of that same body slamming me to the ground during our last training session. My back still hurt.

"Frank, you know this isn't my fault, right?"

"Shut. Up."

I did.

"Where are you?" he asked.

"Heading back your way. Figured we could eat and regroup."

"Eat and regroup? What do you think we're doing out here? Vacationing?" A long pause. "Why the fuck am I stuck with you?" Disconnect.

I hated being hung up on. I debated calling Simon. He'd made clear to me how important finding Evelyn and recovering the money she'd taken was to him. He'd make me feel better, but unless I quit altogether, he wouldn't save me from Frank. If I worked for Simon Pritchard I had to listen to Frank. Do what he asked and learn how to kill as well as he did. For months, I'd endured him and his training method—yelling, "You're too slow. You're too weak. You're not cut out for this." But I was still here. I couldn't quit. I had to prove Frank wrong. I had to find Evelyn Bright.

Somewhere behind the clouds the sun was up. In the overcast light of morning, I found her. Well, her car anyway. I called Frank.

"First, I found her car. Empty car, cold engine. Either she's been picked up by somebody else—and really it's barely daylight, what are the chances of that—or she's walking right now down the same road I'm driving on."

"And second?"

"Oh," I took a breath. "Don't hang up on me. I know you don't like me but I'm trying."

"Did you call Simon and cry to him? Did you tell him I was mean to you again?"

Frank hated when I complained about anything. One more trait that proved I was too soft for this work.

"You don't think I can do this, do you?" I said.

"No."

"I'm going get the money from her."

"How are you going to do that?"

I didn't have a fucking clue. But ammunition, the man didn't need. I said, "You'll see. Get in the car, wait for me to call you. Bye, Frank."

A pause. "Goodbye, Laura."

I smiled. Progress.

***

It wasn't long before I spotted someone walking alongside the highway. It had to be her. Walking with her head down, shoulders hunched against the weather, a duffel bag slung over one shoulder. I called Frank, put the phone on speaker and dropped it in the cup holder. I pulled up alongside her and as she turned to me, I fought to keep recognition out of my face. She was the drowned-rat version of the woman in the photo Frank showed me three days earlier, but it was definitely her.

"Hey, need a ride?" I said.

She looked me over warily. I was twenty-six but looked younger. An All-American black girl, wearing jeans, a zip-up sweatshirt and my best Midwest smile. Was she getting in the car? Hell, yes she was.

"My car broke down a ways back. Can I get a ride to the diner up the road? I have to get out of this weather."

"A diner?" I looked down the sloping road but saw nothing but poles, wires and scattered trees. All of it wet.

"It's not far. It's about three miles away, there's a turn-off for it. Follow the trucks." She had to yell the last part as another truck rumbled past. She tossed her bag in the back, slid into the seat and buckled up. My phone vibrated in its cup holder, the alert that a call had ended. Then it vibrated again. I answered it.

"Hi Dad," I chirped.

"I'm too fucking young to be your dad." Frank was touchy about his age and his hairline. "Look, I'll find you. I'll be at least a half hour. Stall." He hung up.

I kept my end of the conversation going. "I'm fine. I should be there in another day. Bye." I dropped the phone in my lap and returned my hands to the wheel.

"Road trip?" she asked.

"I'm driving home. I'm Laura."

"Jennifer," she lied.

"Glad to meet you, Jennifer. Are you hungry? I'm starved."

She said she was and I offered to buy her breakfast. The overcast sky let loose with a torrent of rain. I cranked the wipers into hyper-drive while I slowed the car down to a crawl. The trucks hauled past us, kicking up more water and dirt. I gripped the wheel.

"I just knew I was going to get hit walking out there but I think it might be worse in the car."

I looked in the rear-view mirror, changed lanes and glanced over at her. Her bobbed black hair was striking against her pale, near translucent skin. I wondered why she stole the money. I guess life with Travis was better than life with a cheating husband. Not that it mattered. I needed to focus.

"We'll get through it," I said.

We pulled into the parking lot of the Hard Brake Diner. The lot was jammed with big rigs. I maneuvered through and found a spot to park on the backside of the diner.

"That was fun," I said. We both laughed. I peeled my hands off the steering wheel, rubbed the feeling back into them.

"Look at that." She pointed to the river rushing past the diner. The water was barely contained within the banks. The feeble excuse for a fence had long since come down. A piece of it trailed in the water.

She shivered. "Let's go have some coffee."

We ran into the diner, drew a few stares but the men at the counters went back to their eggs and coffee. We sat at a booth in the back far enough away from other diners. From our booth we had a view of the rushing water and the dumpsters.

She sat down across from me and said, "God, I'm tired."

"Me too. Drove all day yesterday."

"I've done quite a bit of driving myself lately. But I woke up this morning knowing I had to get a move on. Then that damn car died."

Yeah, that damn car. The only reason I'd caught up with you. "Rotten luck," I said.

"Yeah but I'll get it fixed. Or maybe I'll catch the bus. Don't know. Don't care."

A waitress with Amy written crookedly on her nametag came over and asked if we wanted coffee. We said yes to coffee. Then we ordered and when the food showed up we ate in silence, reveling in the warmth of the food and the diner. A few times, she looked around the restaurant, searching for Travis I assumed. I paid the bill and we had more coffee. Time for business.

"Thanks, honey. You're sweet to do this." She added sugar and cream to her coffee and stirred.

"Hey, no problem, Evelyn."

She stopped stirring her coffee, her eyes flicked upwards and met mine. "No, my name is…"

"You were lying."

She drew in a shaky breath. "Were you?"

"No. My name's Laura." My heart beat faster and I was too warm. I should have taken my jacket off. I'm in control here. Focus. Focus. Focus.

"Right. So you followed me?"

"I wish. But no, we found Travis. He gave you up. We drove all night to get here. But then you weren't at the motel."

I shook my head. Even if I pulled this off and convinced her to give me the money, I would still have to endure extra time in the ring or on the mat with Frank. He seemed to think I needed to know how to box. At five three, I didn't need to know how to box; I only needed to know when to run.

"Travis told you?"

"Don't blame him. Frank can be very persuasive."

She nodded, chewed her lip. "Frank? You have a partner then?"

"Yes." I unzipped my jacket, pushed my coffee away.

"Okay. Which one is he?" She turned to look at the row of truckers at the counter.

"The angry-looking one." That should narrow it down to twelve or so. They sat in a line at the counter, a rainbow of flannel and plaid. They ate and chatted up our waitress Amy, none concerned with us. "I'm kidding. He's not here yet."

She turned back to me. Anger flitted around her eyes but she seemed too tired to bother. I watched her finger her coffee cup, turning an idea over in her head.

"Escaping isn't really an option, Evelyn. I mean, you could try but Frank would just find you. Trust me, dealing with me is better."

Evelyn placed her hands flat on the tabletop. Her pinky finger twitched and began to tap. She kept her eyes down. "So you want the money?"

"I want the money. Frank wants your head." She bit her lip again and I thought she might actually cry. "I was hired to find you, to get rid of you but maybe we can work out a deal."

"A deal?" She leaned forward, eyes locked on my face.

"We're tired. You weren't where you were supposed to be and the beds in the motel where we slept weren't the greatest. Frank has zero patience today. So give me the money and go."

"You'd let me go?" Her eyebrows rose up and disappeared behind her jet-black bangs.

"Look, what's your life worth? Three mil? Once Frank gets here, we're out of options. Tell me where the money is, then get up and walk away."

"Why?"

"Why not?"

I gave her some time to mull over her options. Mine were pretty limited. Frank wasn't here yet but he would be soon. Letting her go was a risk, but the idea of me bringing Simon the missing money was too good to pass up. It would be worth any fallout from Frank. If I pulled this off, he could kiss my ass. The rain was falling heavier now. I turned back to Evelyn. She was watching me.

"How did you get in to this profession?' she asked. "You don't exactly look like the type. I mean, you look like a nice girl."

"I am a nice girl," I said. "But we all make choices and have to live with the consequences. I took the low road and buried someone underneath it." I killed a man. I'd do it again. Some people don't deserve to breathe; he was one who didn't. Killing him wasn't hard. Hell, I was even ready to call the police and confess. But then I met Simon and everything changed.

Evelyn Bright said, "I took this money from my husband."

"I know, but it wasn't his. By the way, your husband? He's dead. Him and the woman he was cheating on you with. But before your husband died, he told us about Travis, the way he was always looking at you. I think he may have been a little jealous. Then the girlfriend called you a bitch. Frank broke her neck. The man has no manners but then he gets upset when she calls you a bitch. He's an enigma." I drank my coffee.

She frowned and looked out the window. "I followed him." Her voice pitched lower now. "I knew something was wrong but I didn't expect her." She frowned and looked back at me. "I never cheated on my husband. Thought about it but didn't do it. Then I saw them together."

"Well, he's paid his price now. Hasn't he?"

"So they're really dead?" Her eyes were wide, her skin impossibly pale under the fluorescent lights of the diner.

"I killed your husband myself," I lied. Frank had done the job. Then he'd pointed at them, the husband and the mistress, and told me that this was how you do the job. Quick and clean. But Evelyn needed to fear me so I figured a little lie might encourage that reaction.

"He was going to leave me. I thought fine, let him go. Then I found the money. Could not believe it." Tears made her eyes glisten and the grin that crept across her face made her look feral.

"Yeah, I bet. Lotta money."

Her hands shook. She clasped them together in front of her cup. "I don't have it all with me."

"I figured. That bag doesn't look like it weighs nearly enough to hold three million dollars. How much is in it?"

"Two hundred thousand."

"And the rest?"

"In a safe deposit box."

"Must be a big box." I produced a pen from my purse and a napkin from the dispenser. I laid them down in front of her. "Your move, Mrs. Bright."

She wiped at the tears. "Maybe you'll kill me anyway. Keep the money for yourself."

"I don't need the money."

"You're young. You could go anywhere on that kind of money. Make a whole new life for yourself. That's what I wanted to do."

"Look I'm gonna be straight with you. The only thing I want is to go home. Home to my bed and my boyfriend. My boyfriend needs the money. All I have to do is prove I'm his good girl. I do this job, prove to him and Frank I can do this and I'll make him happy. I bring home that money. It's a bigger payday for him." Not to mention that he'd keep me in bed for days. Simon might even let me blindfold him again. That was fun.

"He's got you good," she said.

"Is there any other way to be? If so, I don't know it. I'm his."

"And when he's done with you, he'll find somebody new to screw you over with."

Was she really looking to push me? Couldn't she see how good this deal was? I studied her face. She thought she had me. Thought that she, older, smarter, could teach me something about life. "Not every man is your husband Mrs. Bright." I tried to stay even.

"True, some are killers who have their clueless little girlfriends do their dirty work for them."

I looked over at the counter. Only five of the original customers were still there. No one was looking. I swung my arm in a leisurely arc that gained momentum before impact.

Her pretty little head ricocheted off my hand and into the window. I sipped my coffee. A couple of the men turned at the sound but I looked innocent enough and Evelyn was so shocked she had nothing to say yet.

Finally she said, "Aren't you tough? Doesn't change a thing though." She rubbed her cheek.

"This was a one time only offer. A win-win, I thought. I guess we're done." I stood and picked up my purse. I leaned down close to her and whispered, "You won't see him coming. Frank, I mean. Good luck walking out of here."

"Wait." Quickly, she wrote a name and an address.

I dropped back on to the seat across from her and glanced at the napkin. "What is this?"

"A private vault. You pay upfront for a year and you have a locked box with twenty-four-hour access and security."

"Is there a key to this private vault?"

She bit her lip. Deciding, I supposed. She had everything to lose as far as I could see. I could be telling the truth or my partner might grab her as soon as she left. From her pocket she produced key. She dropped them on the table. "There's a code too." She wrote that down.

"That was easy wasn't it?" I smiled. She didn't.

"Are we done here?" she asked.

"Yes. Don't forget your bag. You'll need dry clothes." I handed over the keys to the Jetta. She looked at me. "Frank has a car. Take mine. Be careful though. He stole it, so drive the speed limit. It would suck for this to all go wrong because you couldn't drive sixty-five."

"Your boyfriend. He's going to disappoint you someday. You can't give everything to one man and not expect to be disappointed."

"Thanks for the advice. Here's a little for you. If I find out you're lying to me, if the money isn't there, you'll be seeing me again."

She stood and it was her turn to look down at me. I tried to be the picture of menace and innocence. Something Frank had no trouble in projecting. The man can turn his charm on in an instant if he wants. He can sweet talk nearly as well as Simon. She gave me a little nod, snatched up the car keys and stomped out into the rain. I watched her until she disappeared around the corner of the building.

The waitress came back over.

"Is your friend going to want more coffee?"

"No. She's leaving. I'll take some though."

It was another twenty minutes before Frank showed. He glanced around the diner. He looked wet and unhappy. He walked over and wedged himself into the seat across from me.

"You're late," I said.

"Explain to me why I'm not seeing her?"

"I let her go." My voice almost didn't quaver. Almost.

Frank reached out and I flinched. He picked up my coffee cup and sipped from it. "You drink this without sugar?" He frowned.

I pushed the napkin with the address to the money on it over to him. "Yep, I like it black. Just like me." I didn't even try for a smile.

"Spare me." He tore several packets of sugar open and dumped them in the cup. While he stirred he looked at the napkin. "This is what?"

"She put the money in private vault in San Diego. That's the address and the code."

"You got her to give you the money?"

"I convinced her."

"How?"

"I slapped her and told her if the money wasn't there, we'd be seeing each other soon."

"Laura, if the money isn't there," he stopped, looked at me carefully. His eyes were an odd shade of blue. An electric blue. They analyzed me, took me in and spat me out. "This isn't a game, you know."

"I know."

He leaned forward. "Do you? You act like you don't. You're role-playing. Tonight I'm Simon's girlfriend.

Tomorrow, I'm Laura the assassin." His hand snatched up my wrist and pulled me forward. "People are going to die, Laura, whether we do it or somebody else does it. If you're in this, people will die by your hand." He squeezed hard enough to make tears well up. I yanked my arm away. He sat back in the booth. His hard-eyed look seemed to soften as I rubbed my wrist.

"Let me know if that gives you a problem later," he said. That was a Frank Joyce apology. Crack my rib, give me a concussion then say, "Let me know if that minor to major injury is a problem." I did once, with the cracked rib; he roughed me up worse when it healed. I kept my mouth shut now about injuries.

"I'm fine."

He dropped a tip on the table and headed for the door with me a step behind him. He wasn't nearly as angry as I expected him to be. Which made me wonder why. He started the car and I worked to stay quiet. I failed. Evelyn's comment came back to me again.

"Do you think Simon is using me?" I asked.

"Somebody say that?" I nodded. "He's paying you. Don't worry about it."

"So because he's paying me, he's not using me?"

"Trust me. If anyone's getting used here, it's me."

"How so?"

"I'm the one who has to come with you. Simon's afraid you'll get yourself killed."

"You don't think I will?"

"Cupcake, I don't much care. But Simon does, so you listen to me and you'll always bring that fine ass of yours home to him, okay? This situation you have us in...this makes me unhappy." If there was more to be said, Frank suddenly wasn't interested in sharing. I watched him grip the steering wheel tighter and as we accelerated down the rain-slick highway I wondered what consequences waited for me.

San Diego was a wet place too. We waited until dark and drove up to the building. A plain, white building, with no visible security guards, only a touch pad and a camera next to the door. A plane of tinted glass on either side of the door. More cameras, I figured. A low rumble from Frank.

"I don't like this."

I didn't either but this was my play. If this went wrong, I'd never hear the end of it from Frank. Of course, if this went really wrong, I doubt I'd have to worry about it. I'd be dead or arrested. "I'll go. Park where you can see the front door, okay?"

"The money had better be there."

"It is."

Frank gripped the steering wheel tighter but said nothing. I grabbed the duffel bag Frank had bought from a store on the way to San Diego and got out. I inhaled a lungful of damp air and walked up to the door. I punched the numbers Evelyn had given me into the security pad. A little light next to the door blazed red then shifted to green. The door buzzed and I almost peed my pants. I opened the door and felt the whoosh of cold air. I stepped into an alcove. Another door was directly in front of me. Beside it a sign read: Shut Front Door. Above the door another camera and a red light. I pulled the door shut. The light over the second door changed to green. I pushed it and entered a crypt.

Low lights, marble floors and numbered plaques on walls and around the edge of the floor. It was impressive and creepy. I shifted the bag from shoulder to hand and found the gold plaque with my lucky number. The key poised over the keyhole, I took a moment to think of Simon. His face, the green eyes, his smile, the teeth—perfect and straight. The weight of his body on top of mine. I slid the key in and turned. The door opened and a black box loomed before me. I heaved the box out and nearly dropped it. I heaved it to a table along the wall. The box was smaller than I thought it would be. Maybe fifteen inches square. I swung back the lid and exhaled a thankful prayer. Neat stacks of rubber-banded money, pressed and squeezed in, face up and stacked on theirs sides. I counted the bundles of hundreds as I went. It was all there.

Now I could rub Frank's face in this all the way back to Vegas. I stumbled out into the night and searched the street for Frank. A car pulled out from down the street and coasted up. He popped the trunk and I slung the bag in.

"Was it all there?" he asked when I was buckled in and we were already moving down the empty street.

"Yep. Told you I'd get the money."

"Yeah, next time you can work alone."

I pulled my phone from my pocket and dialed Simon.

"You hear me?" Frank said.

"Yeah, yeah." I listened to Simon's phone ring. Once, twice.

"Laura." Frank braked hard at the stop light. I lurched forward, my body straining against the seatbelt.

"What?" I snapped. The rings went on, then voicemail.

"Next time you're working alone."

I looked at him. His jaw was set. His lips pressed tight together, thin and knife-like. I softened my tone, said, "I heard you."

Frank turned his attention back to the road. The light remained red. I dialed Simon again. Voicemail again. We never left voicemail messages. The phones we carried were cheap, pay as you go phones. We replaced them constantly. Trading phones for each new job, dumping them within days of returning if not in the city we were working in. Simon always answered.

"Did Simon change phones again?"

Frank scowled at me, pulled his own phone out and dialed. The light turned green and he sped out into the intersection. "She wants you," he said into the phone. He handed it to me.

I fumbled his phone, braced a foot on the dashboard and said hello.

"Hey, babe." Simon sounded odd, irritated.

"Everything okay?"

"Yeah, what do you need?"

"To tell you about a two point eight million dollar payday."

"You're fucking kidding me." I could hear his smile, nearly felt it. "Frank got the money?"

"No, I did," I said a little shrilly. I wasn't letting let Frank take the credit for this score.

"Really? I'll be damned." His voice was all sweetness but still there was irritation.

"Yes. And you are damned, same as me. What's wrong?"

He sighed. "Nothing I can get into right now. Come home. Where are you anyway?"

"San Diego. The way Frank's driving, we'll be home tonight."

"Tomorrow," Frank said.

"I heard him. I'll see you then," Simon said.

We drove until the night sky and the desert were indistinguishable. We stopped at the first motel we found. Rooms paid for, I tried to sleep. Periodically, I called Simon. He never answered.

***

The first gambling outpost rose up from the desert, a glimmering landmark against desert and asphalt. We stopped for breakfast—steak and eggs $7.95—and marveled at the different cocktail of waitresses. Varying in ages from the old, white hair dyed Miss Clairol brown, to the youngish disabled, in their thirties and forties, limping along with fallen arches, arthritic knees and carpal-tunnel-plagued wrists, both sets in modest skirts, black nurse's shoes, over-applied mascara and surprisingly genuine smiles. When we were served Frank put his head down and ate like there was nothing more important than the eggs in front of him.

I wanted to poke at his edges. He'd known Simon longer. He'd know what Simon was thinking.

"Frank, what's going on with Simon?"

"Ask your boyfriend." He maneuvered eggs onto the fork and into his mouth.

"I would, only he doesn't seem to want to answer when I call him." Frank shrugged, more food in mouth. "Frank, what don't I know?"

"You're twenty-six, you don't know anything." My objections rolled out of my mouth but he stopped them with a hand. "I'm eating."

I said nothing more. Frank let me drive home while he slept, to avoid the conversation, I was sure. An hour later we were back in Vegas.

***

The house I shared with Simon was tiny. Built in the early railroad days of Las Vegas, these cottages were barely 800 square feet. 2 bedrooms, a sliver of a kitchen, a closet for bathroom and laundry room. I adored it though. I moved in the day Simon and I met. We lived in the bedroom for the most part, slept in our island of a bed and made love in every room of this house. Against every wall, on every counter, on every floor in every room. Since the day he brought me here, I had had him every way I could imagine.

Today was no different. I wanted to talk about the phone calls he hadn't answered and the distance I'd felt lately. But within twenty seconds in the same room Simon had me stripped and pinned to the bed. He worked out all the stress and tension of my last few days in a few short hours.

***

I'd slept for a couple of hours before waking to find him gone. Not unusual for him, leaving before I woke. But when our time apart had stretched to nearly a week, usually we spent the first day back stuck together and horizontal. I checked my phone for a missed call and there was the odd thing. A text message waited for me:

<things have changed i met someone i'll get my stuff later>

***

It was like someone was squeezing the air from my lungs, blood from my veins. I slipped from the bed to the floor. The very same hardwood floors we had put down three months earlier were cool against my cheek and they said nothing about my tears.

At some point the doorbell caught my attention. For a moment I thought it would be him, ready to talk at least, if not fall to his knees and beg forgiveness. But it was Frank.

"What happened?" He stepped forward, looking surprised.

"I don't know," I said. I didn't know. Frank followed me to my couch. I handed him my phone.

"Well, fuck," he said after he read the message. I nodded and cried. He called Simon from my phone but he too received no answer. When he called from his phone, one ring and contact. Frank left me on the couch while he wandered into my kitchen. He came back, drink in hand.

"What's going on?" I asked. "Why is he doing this?" My broken heart had no shame, no fear even when faced with Frank's surly demeanor. Frank held his hand over my eyes then drew it across my forehead and smoothed my hair. This was bad. He was trying to be nice to me.

"Here I was all ready to kick your ass tonight." He looked down at me and sighed.

"I don't understand."

"When you're on this side of it, on the receiving end, you never do. Cupcake, this is not your life. This is just a moment. Look, take some time off. We'll talk later." He put his glass in my kitchen then he was gone.

My cell phone rang again. Frank calling from his car, which was parked in front of my house. My house. Simon's house? Another detail to figure out. I had moved in with him and now he was moving out. I found my shoes, buttoned my jeans, put on a T-shirt, grabbed my hairbrush, my packed overnight bag, and walked out to Frank's car. I didn't make eye contact as I swung my bag into his back seat. I had one leg in the car when he said,

"You look like crap."

I paused, my ass in the seat and one leg still in the street, undecided. I wasn't sure why I was letting him drive me to the airport. I hadn't seen him, or anyone else, for two weeks. Everyone had given me time to myself. I was positive it was Simon calling and hanging up every day. His way of making sure I was still alive.

I gripped the door handle tighter waiting for some flip remark but it didn't come. I pulled my other leg in, shut the door, buckled up and closed my eyes. We were halfway to the airport when he spoke again.

"Did you have a nice vacation?"

"Please don't." Neither my voice nor my body was as strong as it needed to be to fend off Frank.

"Don't what? I'm making conversation."

"Don't be nice to me. You suck at it. Just drive."

The tears were back. No sobbing or hiccupping, just silent running tears. Why was it that Frank always made me feel like a kid? Normally, he'd tell me I was being weak but today, Frank just put a box of tissues in my lap and drove on.

***

I was stuck in Reno—the biggest little city in the world. My connecting flight was delayed due to weather. My cell phone rang.

"So you're delayed, huh?"

I turned away from the floor-to-ceiling windows I'd been staring out of for the last hour, fully expecting to see Frank behind me.

"Yeah," I said. "Where are you?"

"Not behind you, so stop looking," Frank said.

I turned back to my tree-lined view. Reno was pretty. "You ever do any work in Reno?" I asked.

"No and neither will you."

"Why's that?"

"You don't work in your backyard. Your hire somebody from outside to trim your bushes and kill the vermin. Never make that mistake, Cupcake." Ah, Frank's little euphemisms. It was almost comforting.

"Why are calling me?"

"Just making sure you're up for the job."

"Tell him I'm fine."

"I will, if he asks."

"So he hasn't?"

"Focus, Laura. Go to Portland, do the job, and come home. And don't think I won't be expecting you at the warehouse the second after your plane touches down. A few weeks of sitting on your ass probably softened you up again. All that fucking work and now I have to start over." He hung up and I closed my phone. Frank was my teacher of all things violent. Frank's first lesson:

You only get one chance to make a first impression. When in a fight, throw the first punch, make it a cheap shot, and don't forget to kick them when they are down.

22

The warehouse was where Frank regularly inflicted damage on me. Teaching me the way of his world. Now with the recent developments, he seemed to be trying to help me navigate this new version of my world. My bereft new world.

The woman Simon left me for was quite a bit taller than me I was told. His secretary Maybellyne had been giving me all the info I could want. I guess the new girlfriend was connected. And pretty…beautiful more likely. Simon had a pretty girl in me. If he was trading in, he was trading up. He wouldn't settle for an equivalent model. My replacement was beautiful, tall, blonde and white. Me: short and black and pretty average. What burned was that she was fucking him and I just got to cry on his button-down shirts. The nice ones I bought him for his birthday. The ones he left behind.

***

My flight was finally ready to go. Soon I would get to inflict some pain on someone else. Frank said it would be good for my psyche. He was a sick man. But I was his trainee so what did that make me?

Todd Johansson gambled and owed the wrong type of people. The impatient type. Todd failed to pay and now he was bleeding out in his bathroom.

Todd had surprised me though. Instead of being in his bed sleeping, he was in his bathroom answering an early morning call of nature when I stepped into his rented home. I checked his kitchen and found an eight-inch chef's knife in the knife block. I waited just outside the bathroom door, the knife in one hand and my telescoping baton in the other.

When he exited he caught sight of me and didn't hesitate, he just swung. Todd was six three, two hundred thirty pounds; I was lucky he missed. I caught him full in the face with my baton, which drove him back into the bathroom. While he was busy holding his nose and hollering his outrage, I dropped the baton and stepped in with the knife. But Todd recovered quickly and grabbed my hand and twisted the blade away. I pulled back. He moved with me still hollering and cussing. The bathroom was too narrow for me to get any power behind my swing but I tried to hit him in the face again. He grunted but he held me tight. He squeezed my wrist trying to get me to let go of the knife, tried to pull it from my hand. But with gloves on, I had the better grip.

I tried a different tactic and pushed forward with all my weight. He shoved me back. My heel hit the door frame and I stumbled. I nearly fell but Todd's body pushed me into the wall. The breath rushed out of me and Todd still holding the knife in his hand bashed me into the wall until I let it go. I fell, dazed, to the floor.

He stood over me breathing hard. I blinked trying to focus on him. He stepped back into the bathroom. Sat down heavy on the toilet. He mumbled. "Can't believe this." I heard the knife clatter to the floor. And then he was silent.

I sat there looking at him. He'd lost a slipper. I must have stabbed him when he shoved me against the wall.

"Fuck me," I said. How lucky did I just get? I sat watching him for long time. Just to make sure.

I scooped up my baton but left the knife where it was. When I thought I could stand and not wobble I went to his kitchen sink, peeled the gloves off and checked for cuts. None to be found luckily. I stowed the gloves and the baton in the small backpack I wore then I went to his small living room.

The previous day's sport scores were centered on his small plywood coffee table. I sat gingerly on his denim-covered couch and lifted the newspaper to see what Lady Luck had given him for the day. Really, the stats were indecipherable to me.

Under the sports section were more papers. Divorce papers. His wife had left him. Maybe she was tired of the lies he surely told; the money that never seemed to make it home. Maybe she found someone else.

My backpack vibrated. I dropped the papers, took the backpack off and dug in a side pocket for the phone. Simon's number flashed on the display. I let my finger hover over the accept button. Closed my eyes and let the memory of his voice warm me. His words always came slow. Easy.

Fuck him. I hit reject and closed the phone. I dropped it on the table and sat back on Todd's couch. Cool air seeped in through the window edges. The phone buzzed again. I watched it shimmy on the newspaper. It stopped. Then began its dance again. I picked up and saw a number I didn't recognize.

I hit accept and listened. There was a moment of silence. Then Frank was yelling, "Laura! Where the fuck are you? Tell me you haven't gone yet."

I leapt up like he was in the room. "What? I'm already here, Frank. I'm done."

"Get out."

"What? Why?"

"Just do it now."

I hung up, grabbed my pack and ran for the back door. My hand trembled on the doorknob but I did manage to remember to look before I ran out. Through the back door's window I could see the yard and the fence that surrounded it. Directly behind the fence was an alley. Once in the alley, I could run for blocks and hardly be noticed. It was how I'd gotten here.

A quarter moon hung high in the sky. Not much light but enough. I was clear to the fence. I slipped out, closed the door behind me. Todd's back porch creaked with my weight, the stairs even more so. A flagstone path led to the hinged door in the fence. I was nearly there when the gate swung open.

The man before me looked as startled as I felt. Yet he managed to speak before I found my voice.

"Hello."

"Hi," I said.

"Leaving? Todd's not home?" He was dressed like I was, in all black.

"Todd? Wrong house. If you could just let me," I pointed and half stepped towards the gate. He grabbed my wrist, pulled me forward, and then punched me in the face. My knees gave out but he held me up. "Try again."

I dropped the backpack and swung but he spun me around, twisting my arm behind my back and yanking it up high. The pain brought tears to my eyes and I was helpless to prevent them from running down my face.

"Fuck."

"Now is Todd in that house?" he asked.

I nodded.

"Asleep?" He sounded so hopeful, like his date might still be waiting. A courting hitman.

I couldn't help my grin.

"Permanently," I said.

He released me with a push. I stumbled and landed hard on my twisted arm. The jolt of pain made me yelp.

"Somebody paid you to kill him?" He leaned down over me. I nodded again. I didn't have a clue how to get out of this. He threw his hands up. "Fuck. What is this world coming too?" Poor disappointed hitman. He took a step closer and the limp light from the moon illuminated a deep scar that ran from his upper lip to the ear. "I do this for a living, you know? What are you doing? Interning? Did you fail your college boards and now you're temping as a contract killer?"

I levered myself to my feet. "I'm sorry that I got here first. No harm done."

"Yeah," he turned his back to me, hands finger-locked behind his head. "I suppose."

I edged slowly past him, picking up my backpack as I went. Frank's warning to get out blared in my head. Get out. Get out. Get out. Fuck Frank, I'm trying.

"Only I came all the way out here to kill somebody. Guess you'll have to do."

He spun on me, gun already out and finger on the trigger. Only I wasn't where he thought I'd be. I whipped the bag at him and rolled left. He missed. On my feet again I stayed low and tried to take him down by tackling his legs. He grunted but stayed up, whacking me with the butt of his gun and I fell away. His fist connected with my face again and again. Then he was kicking me and I just curled up.

I waited for the bullet. I heard a sound and the next blow never landed. Something hit the flagstone near my head. I opened my eyes. The gun was inches from me. Four feet away, two figures collided with the fence and each other. My jilted hitman, broken up over a wasted trip, fell heavy against the fence. It shook but held. He kicked out, tripping the other. The other, Frank, fell. I picked up the gun, swayed up onto my knees and with my uninjured eye, aimed, sighted and squeezed the trigger three times in rapid succession. The hitman dropped.

Frank rose to his feet, breathing heavy. He crossed to me and held out a hand. I released my grip on the gun and let it fall into his big hand. He turned back to the downed man, fired two more shots into him. He wasn't getting up again.

"Come on," Frank said.

I limped out of the yard behind Frank. We walked in silence to his car. Once in and safely down the road, he said, "You okay?"

I was bleeding. I could feel my face swelling. The heat and tightness of the skin that was damaged and bruised. External representation of my broken heart.

"No."

He nodded. "You will be. Later."

Back in Vegas I spoke with Simon over the phone. He wanted to see me but Frank was a large obstacle to overcome. He took the phone from me. The one-sided conversation was heated and ended with, "You brought her in, but I made her." After he hung up he told me all about how many people Todd had pissed off and how many people wanted him dead. They were angry enough to hire other killers and there were two others who I had beaten to the kill.

"Be careful, Cupcake. You're gonna make a name for yourself." With that he left me again to walk around my tiny, empty house and lick my wounds.

6

Simon and I met over a dead body. The dead man was Jimmy MacAvoy, Jimmy Mac, to those who loved and loathed him. My best friend Fiona adored the son of a bitch.

I'm not sure when I knew she was gone. She made excuses for the college classes she missed and the phone calls she stopped returning. One day she was there, and then the days she was gone stretched out to form weeks then months.

I searched all the Las Vegas bars and strip clubs where I thought she might be. Checked hospitals and the county morgue too. A hundred girls in each location could have been her. The glossy shiny club girls looking fierce in platform heels; their battered and bruised versions, the wisp-thin drug waifs, and their final versions—Jane Does lining morgue shelves waiting for their families to come for them; more likely settling for the county's good graces and dedicated tax money when their families didn't come. A hard earth burial in the city of neon illusions.

I found her in a motel. Fiona opened the door, saw me and skittered away. Jimmy sat on the edge of the bed, red-faced, shirt off, pants unbuckled, waiting to be serviced. She looked too thin and sallow-skinned to not be on something. Jimmy, looking far too healthy in comparison, patted the bed.

"Nice to see you. Come sit. Fiona would love you to stay."

Fiona stood across the room from me. Her brown eyes looked too big for her face. Her fine brown hair hung lifeless around her face. "You shouldn't have come," she said.

"Fi, come with me."

"I'm okay." She walked over to me and wrapped her arms around me. She was trembling. Her voice was low and conspiratorial as she whispered, "Tell my mom I'm okay. Let me go. I'm fine here with Jimmy."

To my undying shame, I did. I left her alone. She was dead two weeks later. It was a week before they found her. It was the smell that alerted them. Funny thing, Jimmy was nowhere to be found. Not on the registration but someone had paid up for a full month.

Declared an overdose, there was nothing to do but take her home and I did. As they shoveled the Illinois earth over her casket I begged for forgiveness and swore vengeance. Then I came back to Vegas.

***

Jimmy Mac loved the hen houses. Three or four times a week he would head out down the road out of town to visit the legalized prostitutes. I borrowed a car and followed Jimmy on one of his hen runs. I knew it would be dark when he headed back. Drunk and probably high, he would drive back and I would be waiting. I didn't have some great plan. I waited until I saw him walk out of the establishment then I drove far enough down the road and put up the hood. A brown wig styled to cover my face somewhat, a short skirt, heels and a warm smile. I walked back and forth with my cell phone up to my ear pantomiming aggravation. He drove past me and nearly wrecked his car stopping and turning. He got out waving.

"Hey there. You need some help?" Even from six feet away I could smell the alcohol on him. I kept my face turned away from him while he assessed my legs and ass in the headlights.

"Yeah, something is wrong with the engine, I think. Could you look at it?" I giggled and my stomach turned over.

He patted my ass. "Sure, honey. Get in and turn it over when I tell ya." He was much drunker than I anticipated. He went to the engine and I slipped into the driver's seat. From between the seat I pulled the short-handled kitchen knife I had bought a few weeks back. I slipped my shoes off and got out. I came around the other side and while he bent down pulling on this and that, I crept up and leaned in close to him.

"Hey, Mahogany, get back in the car and turn the engine over." He turned to me. I held his eyes. Then recognition turned his smile from predatory to a contorted sneer. "Well, if it isn't Fiona's little friend. What do you think you're doing, little girl?"

I said nothing. He glanced down at the knife.

"Did you think you were going to get me to confess to killing little Fi? She did herself in. Too bad you couldn't join us when she was alive. The three of us could have had us some fun." Then he smiled, "But you'd never do that, would you?"

He laughed then. Mistakenly thinking I wasn't a threat to him. I stepped in close to him, close enough to get his whole scent—aftershave, sweat, sex and alcohol. Then I stabbed him, repeatedly. His laughter stopped. A gurgle rose from his throat and spilled out dark across his chin. Blood. He went to his knees and I let him fall, the knife wedge firmly in his chest where the last blow had landed. I stood over him, waiting to see the spark of life leave his eyes.

"No, Jimmy, I'm not a nice girl."

His last breath wheezed out. I didn't care if I was caught and convicted. Fiona was avenged. My friend could rest.

I didn't hear the car coming up behind me but the squeal of brakes drew me from my crouched position to see who was stopping. Another black SUV backed up and around behind my car. A man got out and jogged over to me. His face looked ghostly pale in the headlights from Jimmy's vehicle. He looked from me to Jimmy Mac, dead on the ground. He looked at me again.

"What happened?"

"He killed my friend," I said. Then I began to cry. The man gathered me in his arms and held me a moment.

"Look, we have to get out of here. You okay to drive?"

I shook my head no. "Call the police." I mumbled into his chest.

"No, honey we have to go. You drive and I'll follow you okay?" I nodded. He placed me in the driver's seat and I started the car.

"I'm Simon, by the way."

"Laura."

"Well, Laura, do me a favor and don't run over the bastard." He smiled at me and the world snapped into focus again. I smiled back. We drove away. Clean.

I'd been Simon's ever since.

7

It was raining in Denver when I arrived. A good sign. Bad weather meant less chance of being identified. The guy I was looking for, Joe, was checked in at the Liberty Motel. I watched him leave his room and walk down the street to the Roseweed Bar. I followed and parked my car. I spent long minutes checking the parking lot.

Simon wanted to send me here with Frank. I told him I didn't need a babysitter anymore. Besides, hadn't I killed and gotten away clean before? To his credit, he didn't mention that he helped me get away the first time. It wouldn't be out of character for him to send someone to follow me. Cars were lined up, but no one lingered out here in the rain. I ran into the bar.

Music blared but it couldn't overwhelm the rumble of conversation and laughter. I shook the rain off my coat and hair. I spotted Joe across the room at the jukebox. I hadn't decided how I was going to complete my task, but I decided that watching him for a little while might give me an idea. I grabbed a beer from the bar and meandered in his direction. My intention was to stake out a booth or corner away from the bulk of the party crowd, but as I passed him, he glanced up, did a double take at me and grinned. The look on his face stopped me dead. It wasn't recognition I saw, but blatant interest...in me.

"Hello." He turned his body my direction and leaned against the machine. He looked me over quickly then his eyes returned to my face and stayed there. The picture I had been provided was of an unremarkable man grinning awkwardly at the camera. The man at the jukebox was handsome. He was one of those people that a freeze-frame moment didn't do justice to.

"Hi." I hadn't felt shy in ages but his lingering gaze balled up my confidence and tossed it in the garbage. He wanted to buy me a drink. He led me to a booth in the back and we sat, traded names, and talked about nothing while assessing each other.

When Simon gave me the vitals—name and place of residence—of the second man I killed, I asked why. Why this man? Did he hurt someone? Did he owe someone? Simon just looked at me, then reached across his desk and called Frank into his office. He lumbered in and hovered over us both, cracking his knuckles. I flinched and touched my leg where a bruise served as my reminder from our last training session. In an old warehouse, Frank tossed me around like a rag-doll four days a week, ostensibly to toughen me up but more likely to demonstrate why I shouldn't piss him off.

"She wants to know why," Simon said to him. Frank grunted as he reached for the paper that contained the vitals. I watched his eyes as they flicked over the information. He crumpled the paper and tossed it back on Simon's desk.

"Because Simon says. Because we have been paid. Because like your mama told you all your baby years, because. These people don't want to be questioned about their reasons."

Frank went with me on that assignment watching the street as I slipped into an unsuspecting man's house and killed him in his sleep. After we got back, he said, "It's not honest work. But nothing is anymore." He pointed a meaty finger in my face, "You screw up out there, it comes back on me. I trained you. Don't ask questions. Don't slip up. They kill people who ask too many questions. I would hate to see you dead." The look he gave me said that it would be him to silence me if I asked any more questions.

I wondered what Joe had done to deserve a death sentence. Nothing about him stood out. He rode in the rodeo circuit. A native Texan, an all-American boy: light brown eyes, sandy blond hair, sideways smile and dimples. His arms were clean, so drugs were probably out though shooting up could be done other places, and I felt a strong need to inspect those places. He had money though he didn't seem to be to flush with cash, or strapped for it either. So he probably didn't owe any. He looked healthy. He looked good, too good. It's too bad someone wanted him dead.

He grinned at me and fetched two shots of tequila. When he returned, he took my hand and licked a wet stripe on it. I laughed and shivered. He sprinkled salt on my hand and slid my shot to me. Normally, I took my tequila straight, no salt, and no chaser but after watching him lick my hand, I reconsidered the whole idea of licking and drinking. Possibilities of drinking now and licking later ran unbidden through my mind. I thought I had discovered a weakness for cowboys, or at least for Texas boys: all white smiles, weathered faces, lean bodies and jeans, just tight enough. Together we downed our shots and followed with the lime chaser. The rest of the drinks went down just as easy and I didn't mind when he kissed me softly.

I said, "Thanks Texas Joe." Then I slipped my hand behind his head and pulled him in for another kiss.

"Aren't you something?" he said, grinning.

"Why yes, I am." I giggled. I was so tilted. Bad, Laura, bad.

Worse, we went back to his hotel room.

8

The rain had gone from being a light shower to an ark-worthy deluge during our time in the bar and we were soaked by the time we made it back to his room. We took our shoes off and I peeled out of my wet coat and dropped it next to my purse on the floor. Foreplay. Between the kissing, he asked what I did. I stripped his shirt off him.

"Tonight, it's you," I said and he kissed me hard.

"I bet," he looked at me closely, "you are a teacher. High school. You drive all the teenage boys wild." He leaned against me, I fell back against the mattress, and he began to strip me. Slowly. Pulling my T-shirt off and dragging it along my chest and down my thighs. He unbuckled my belt making some comment on the size of it. It's heavy and brass-colored. I didn't mention it's my favorite belt because of that buckle. Heavy and painful, one or two men had woken up to the aftermath of that buckle. He slid it off me and I heard it drop to the floor. My jeans came down. He trailed his fingers lightly down my legs, back over my stomach to my bra where he drew lazy figure eights over the lace and between my breasts.

There was an easiness here in this bed that I hadn't known before. All the others had been hurried and dominating, but Texas Joe took his time, and I enjoyed his attention.

"Stay here a second."

Where was I going to go? He crossed the room and rummaged in his suitcase. He produced two silk scarves and

36

returned to me smiling. I smiled uncertainly back at him. I scooted to the head of the bed, suddenly feeling too exposed in my underwear.

He crawled up next to me and stroked my wrist. "Worry not, Ma'am. They're just for fun."

I let him encircle one wrist with the silk. He straddled my legs and kissed me while he wrapped the silk around a corner of the headboard. He reached for the other wrist.

"One is enough I think." I didn't want to spoil this potential fun but a wave of uneasiness had shot through me. "You know, I need to use the bathroom."

And the all-American boy's face descended from angel to demon.

"No." And he slapped me hard across the face. I tasted blood where my teeth had cut my lip. He leaned into my face, "You're not going anywhere. We're gonna have some fun."

I blinked. Tears had sprung up and left trails down my cheeks. I leaned my head back as if resigning myself to this fate. He tasted my tears with a wide swipe of his tongue. Steeling myself for the coming pain, I whipped my head to the side, catching his face with the side of my head. He grunted in surprise. I head-butted him again, catching his nose with the hardest part of my skull. The cartilage gave way and I felt a warm spurt across my chest. He was reeling back and I bucked like the bulls he rode. Fuck eight seconds. He was on the ground bleeding in three. The roar I heard terrified me but I realized it was me yelling like that. I yanked at the scarf, trying to free my hand. Lucky for me he hadn't had the chance to tighten it. I grabbed my belt, wrapped the leather around my hand and cracked him across his face and headed with it. I ran for my clothes. He grabbed for my ankle. I crawled away from him. His face was a bloody mess.

"Stupid fucking whore. Just like the others." Blood spat my direction with every syllable.

He said others. Oh, fuck me. I could guess now why he was supposed to die. Nothing like a good-looking rapist—or worse—to ruin a good night of drinking. I kicked him. Missed, but he was in enough pain to flinch back from me. I scrambled up and got to my clothes and purse. He staggered upright just as I made it out the door and into the pouring rain. No one was in the parking lot of the motel. No one to help me. Scratch that, no one to help him. The street was fifty yards away; the bar we left was another half block down that street. Between the street and me was a vending machine. I ran and hid behind it. I dropped my clothes and pulled out my weapons. Texas Joe crashed out of his room barefoot. I heard his footsteps on the concrete, the splashes of water displaced as he crept along.

"Here kitty." He called for me. Fear had me twitching. I wanted to run. Stupid instinct, fight or flight. I had a job to do.

I flicked my wrist and my telescoping baton extended to full length. With the near silent clicks of the descending rod, I felt calm wash over me. I stepped out in front of him. He was ten feet from me. His eyes flicked to my baton. He leered at me, then came after me. I lunged, swinging the baton. The blow landed across his throat bringing him up short. He slipped on the wet pavement and went down hard. I slipped too and went down on one knee, my upper body landing on a car's hood. He rolled back up and sprang at me. If he got a hand on me, I wouldn't get away again. In my other hand was a little four-inch between-the-fingers beauty of a knife, a gift from Frank.

I was aiming for his throat when I snagged his eye with the blade. A howl erupted from his mouth and I kept at him. I cut his throat and listened:

The rain,

Bar sounds from down the street,

His thick, wet sputters of last breaths, rising up from the ground. Then nothing.

My knees gave out and I crawled back for my clothes. I got dressed and on unsteady legs, walked back to the bar and to my car.

I ran my tongue over the cuts in my mouth. Damn. What was wrong with me? I needed to call in and tell Frank just how I screwed up. With any luck, the police would believe Joe died in a drunken brawl. Luck. I needed some luck. I found the car keys, and started the engine.

Frank would want to talk to me. Something told me it was going to be a conversation to remember.

9

I was the only woman who worked out at Josef's Boxing Palace. The other women there waited on boyfriends and looked at me with distaste. The men they waited for were in varying stages of fitness and power, some tall and lean, others stocky and bulky. One in particular, a boxer with cauliflowered ears, always slowed down when he walked past me, but he'd never spoken to me. All the men here, twenty-seven in total, pretend to ignore me.

When I walked by them, when we were face to face, I was translucent—a ghost, an apparition in sports bra and shorts. Their eyes flicked over my face and lingered on aspects of my body but slipped off to the left or right when I looked back at them. I felt their eyes on me every minute of every hour I spent in that gym. They'd heard something about me. That girl, always with her ear buds in. Josef had told them to behave themselves around me. To leave me alone. I was Frank's protégé. Some of them knew Frank's history; most assumed they knew what Frank did. An enforcer. A local thug. Which made me, what? they wondered. I wondered too. But nobody fucked with Frank, so nobody fucked with me.

The last gym was different. I had shown up, paid some dues and said nothing about who I was or who I worked for. In the end, I complained to Frank that I spent more time evading offers of sex in the alley than I spent actually trying to improve my fighting. So we moved me on and Frank, tired of beating me up himself, loaned me out to Josef. Nice man, thick accent. Big, wide hands that always managed to find an ass cheek when he was trying to help me.

"You must stay on the balls of feet. Like this." His hands grabbed my waist and lifted me until I was on tiptoe, then he lowered me back down. "Balance from here. Move from here." He patted my ass and smiled his blinding smile. He got a deal on tooth whitening last month he told me proudly. I didn't mind him. My punches were better, stronger. I was doing better. Josef didn't make me flinch like Frank did. Where he liked to be close, Frank liked to intimidate.

My ear buds were in but I didn't always listen to music. Most of time I listened to the sounds in the gym. The men were focused. I was focused. The sound of our gloves hitting mitts, hitting heavy bags, hitting flesh made an odd kind of music, the rhythm for the day's workout. I stayed at the heavy bag for hours, trying to find the sweet part of this boxing science. Trying to figure out how to hit harder, better, with the least amount of effort. Josef says the best fighters didn't punch someone they punched through them. Step in when you throw the punch, he told me.

Really, I wanted a good knife and an opportunity to hurt someone. After my last job, Frank was not too keen on letting me out of his sight. Whatever. What's the worst that could happen? I would die?

I lost Simon in the space of a weekend. Really, in just one decisive cut. If you could call a text message decisive. One clean, sharp point to the heart and it was over. I was speechless, breathless. It was a clean cut. Bloodless. Like when you lost a limb. But wasn't there always a little blood? Even in the remains, leaking out slowly. Nobody got away clean.

There was a stutter in the flow of sound. Gloves stopped moving. People stopped talking. I glanced around. At the door, a backlit figure stood surveying the room. Then he moved through and another two men entered. One of the gym employees trotted back to where Josef's office was. The new arrivals, two older men and a kid, early twenties I figured, walked around. They spoke to each other but not to anyone else. Josef emerged from the back. His arms spread wide in welcome, his voice boomed across the newly-quiet gym. He shook hands with the kid, evidently a young stud by the way the men stepped behind him giving him way and control of the conversation. I returned to my bag. I pushed play and House of Pain's *Jump Around* kicked off and I gave the bag a push.

The big bag swung away and I swung too. Before me stood Jimmy Mac, a dead man that still haunted me on occasion. More often, he was the bull's eye I aimed for when I trained. I aimed for his fat, soft middle. My punch was weak, mistimed, the bag already swinging toward me when my padded fist made contact. Jimmy laughed at me and my wrist began to ache. Another ten minutes and I was done. No heart in this today. I put my fists against the nearest wall, arms outstretched, and hung my head. Eyes closed, I rotated my shoulders, flexed and rolled the muscles in my back.

"Is your God listening?" The voice was low and amused. I turned to see the Young Stud.

"What are you talking about?"

"You looked like you were praying."

"Why would I do that?" I leaned back against the wall.

"Pray?" He shrugged. "Some pray for a better right hook and faster feet. Others pray for strength to win their fight." He tilted his head. "You believe in God, don't you?'

"I don't think I've ever considered it."

"It's not possible you've never thought about God." He shifted, folded his long arms across his chest and slouched, his legs splayed apart, settling in. Frank walked up behind him.

"Sure it is," I said.

"Your parents. What religion are they?" He seemed fascinated with me. Frank looked him up and down. Nodded his head in apparent approval, then stepped in between us. Young Stud frowned slightly.

"Cupcake," Frank said to me.

Young Stud drew himself up to his full height. Frank did the same. Frank was the shorter by three inches, but his smile made up the difference with its tinge of menace.

"Well, it was nice talking to you," Young Stud said then walked away.

"Sorry to interrupt," Frank said.

"You aren't and you weren't," I said.

"You can sure pick 'em. Damn, he's tall. See the arms on him? Might have to put a few on the fight."

We walked to the locker room. Two guys stood talking but the conversation ended when they saw Frank.

"He has a fight coming up?" I asked, sliding past the guys. I found my locker, opened it and sat on the bench that ran between the rows.

Frank sat on the bench, said, "Let me see your hands." I presented them. He pulled at the Velcro edge of the wrap and began to unwind it. "Wrist hurt?"

"A little."

"It should. Josef let you wrap your hands? You fucked it all up."

I ignored this. "So the kid has a fight coming up?"

"You really don't know who he is, do you? James Vicario. He could be the next something. At least they're talking him up that way."

"Sounds like he's all hype."

"Maybe. But his record is impressive."

He unwound one hand, letting the tape spool on the bench between us. He probed my wrist, massaging it, twisting it until I tried to yank it from him.

"Relax."

"It's fine," I said.

He grabbed my other hand and repeated the process. Around us the locker room grew silent, the occasional rasp of fabric then the near silent opening and closing of the locker rooms door. Everyone had cleared. Five minutes flat.

"So he wants to see you."

"Oh. What for?"

"I told him you were busy."

"Doing what?"

"Healing from your last beating in the ring. So tomorrow because I covered for you, be in that ring."

"I'll go see him. It's not a problem."

He scoffed. "Whatever. Have your ass in the ring five a.m."

"Five a.m.? I need my beauty sleep. Six?"

"Four thirty. And if you ain't here I will begin the session by dragging you out of bed and then from your house."

I flinched. "His house."

"Fuck. Fine his house or from wherever you reside at. I will beat your ass there again when you get in the ring. Agreed?"

"Yes Frank."

"Good girl. Now go talk to your ex. You two are starting to piss me off."

"I didn't do anything."

"I know, Cupcake." He grabbed me by the ponytail and tugged gently. "That's the problem."

Then he left me to alone. I changed into my jeans, a T-shirt, and sneakers and headed out past the boxers—the wannabes and gonnabes alike.

10

Pritchard Investigations was housed in a mostly empty office building off Sahara Avenue. Built for a national bank's headquarters, it had attracted a few high-dollar tenants—land developers mostly and it had attracted Simon Pritchard. So now he had a very nice office on a floor with no one else on it for the moment. He felt legit. It was obvious in the way he spoke to me.

"Glad you came. Frank was concerned."

He gestured at the chairs in front of his desk. I sat. He leaned forward and placed his hands on his desk.

"You wanted to see me. I work for you so here I am."

"I want you to understand that I know I was wrong in how I dealt with you. It wasn't fair. It wasn't nice either. You deserved better."

The hardest thing about looking at Simon was knowing when to stop. I knew every inch of his body. Had traced it with my tongue, had it pressed up against me so many times I'd lost track. I wish I knew the exact number. Then I could calculate the number of hours we'd spent in bed together. His full lips were pouty. He broke my heart and now he was miserable. Right.

"Okay. Is that all?" I stood up. His gaze held steady on my face then he gave a sigh and looked me over. I tried not to preen.

"No, that's not all, Laura."

I moved around his desk. It was cherry wood. I ran my finger along its side. I placed a hand on it and gave it a shove. It didn't move. "Nice desk. Sturdy." I smiled at him, he laughed.

"Frank said you were fine but I didn't...I needed to see you."

"You've seen me. I'm good."

"Have you given any thought to leaving?"

I turned away from him to look out his large windows and leaned against his desk.

He was saying, "This place wouldn't be the same without you. Pritchard Investigations is doing well and that is, in part, due to you."

I turned back to him, leaned over and touched the lapel of his suit jacket. "You get a better cut of suit, an office with a view of the city, and a better class of girlfriend and now you're all corporate. Shame on you, Simon." He grabbed my hand, stood and pulled me closer. He was nearly a foot taller than me so I had to lean back against the desk to look up at him.

"I never wore a bad suit."

That was true. Nothing looked bad on him. "Can I have my hand back?"

"Answer the question."

"Where would I go, Simon?"

He brought his left hand up to rest on the back of my neck. "You belong here. Don't ever doubt that."

"You have her. Why do you need me?"

"Laura, none of this could have happened without you."

"So it's my fault you dumped me."

His forehead creased when he frowned. "This is not about you and me. This office has done more legitimate work in the past six months than we did the last three years. You helped build this place. You and me and Frank."

He'd moved even closer, our legs were pressed together. His lips were moving but all I could register was the smell of his cologne and the feel of his leg against my own.

"Laura."

I looked him in the eyes. His relaxed a little. He released my hand but the grip on my neck remained, though it was loose.

He said, "It was a lucky thing me finding you. You don't belong anywhere else but here, with me."

But I wasn't with him, though with the look he was giving me and the fact that two inches was all that was separating us, I thought I knew how this might go. Eight weeks was not long enough to forget how we fit together. If he put his hand on my hip now, we'd close the distance. My hand would slip around the back of his neck. One kiss then on the floor and rug burns.

Friction, friction. Spark. Conflagration.

But of course, the phone on the desk bleated. Startled he let my neck go, leaned further into me and hit the speaker phone.

"Marjorie is here to see you. I wasn't sure if you were done with you meeting."

"Another minute." He hung up but kept himself in my personal space. "Did you come straight from the gym?"

I tensed up. "Yeah."

"I figured. You smell like you've been keeping the company of too many men."

I pushed away from him and headed for the door.

"Hey, I didn't mean you smelled bad," he said.

I waved him off. "That speech of yours. How long did you practice it? That bit about me belonging here. It's a nice theory."

"It's not a theory. It's a fact."

"It's a theory until it's tested."

I left his door open when I left. I kept my gaze forward and only waved at his secretary as I left. My replacement sauntered past me in an elegant suit and very high heels.

***

The next morning, Frank had me pinned against the ropes and his fists were coming at me fast. I knew he was pulling his punches, not really wanting to hurt me but I kept trying to back up all the same. He had always insisted that I learn how to fight. He'd told me time and again how one day I was going to be without him to save my ass and then what? I told him I was a fast runner; he made me run in 110-degree heat until I dropped. "At some point, Cupcake, you're gonna have to stop running." he said while looking down at me from the driver's seat of his car.

Nowhere to run now. I blocked one punch, threw one of my own and tried to push him back with a kick to his torso. He grimaced, caught my descending leg and yanked it. My head fell back on the ropes and whipped forward. Then I was on my back and dazed. I was late this morning and he knew why and he wasn't happy about it. So we were arguing.

"Can we not have this discussion again? Please." I mumbled from the floor. My head felt thick and heavy.

He bent down next to me, sweat poured off his face. "What is it about him that you can't get over, Laura? Face it, he dumped you for her. Move on."

"Fuck you." I sat up. The room didn't spin. A good sign, I thought. I walked slowly over to my corner, leaned against the ring post then decided that sitting was better. I slid down and sat facing him. He lumbered over and squatted down next to me, not looking at me but looking out over my shoulder into the gym.

"You gonna answer my question?"

His profile was such that I wondered just how many times his face had been slammed into unforgiving objects. His eyes were set deep back but were such a brilliant blue, the combination made you want to both look closer and get away.

"You think I like watching you fall apart every time you see him?" he whispered low.

"I don't fall apart." I didn't fall apart. I got very drunk.

"Again." Josef called from his seat at ringside.

He sighed. Poor put-upon hired killer. "Come on, Cupcake. Come hurt me." He walked to other side of the ring, crouched down low and smiled the smile that never reached his eyes. The come-on-fuck-with-me smile he usually saved for more threatening people than me. Under my breath I was chanting my new mantra: He is a threat. I have to put him down.

But this was Frank. The one person I would rather run from than fight. This was gonna hurt me.

Josef rang the bell.

Frank launched himself at me like a bear after his dinner. With less enthusiasm, I met him. I faked left and managed to slip by him, landing a blow to his side. He gasped and stumbled a step, but he was fast. He spun and one gigantic paw nearly caught my face. I stepped away then back in again. I aimed for the same side. If I brought him down to my level I'd have a chance. But I didn't have a chance. The blow that connected with my head rocked me backwards and I had enough time to think:

Shit.

And I was on the ground. The mat was rough against my cheek. I heard Josef speaking to me. I blinked him into focus and he smiled at me. Then I spotted Frank with his hand outstretched to touch. I flinched away. Something flickered across his face then he receded from my view and I concentrated on the cool mat under my face.

"You aren't supposed to walk into my fist, Cupcake," he said. Now he was out of the ring and behind me, talking to me through the ropes.

"I know," I said trying to sit up. I spat out the mouth guard and the blood in my mouth.

Josef was next to me, pulling at my shoulder.

"I'm okay, Josef." I batted his hands away, blinking still. One of Josef's boys came ringside waving a cell phone at us. "Frank," he said,

Saved. I slunk out of the ring and found a nearby wall to support me. For twenty minutes I sat there willing the noise to abate. Then I figured out the gym was just filling with people. I closed my eyes and breathed in the scent of the gym. Sweat and musk and leather. The intoxicating scent of the male. I opened my eyes to see the young stud, James, crossing the room. He stood in front of me.

"That was some hit you took," James said.

"You saw that?"

"Yes. You seem okay."

"I am." And I would be after about three days of sleep. My neck hurt looking up at him. I looked at his legs. They looked strong, if a little skinny. A long scar wrapped around one leg, crossing his knee and disappearing underneath his shorts.

"Sit down, will you?"

He sank down next to me. I asked about the scar.

"Skateboarding." He laughed. "My first and only attempt at it."

"Damn, what did you do?"

"Hanging with some friends a few years back. They had a ramp set up on the street in front of a friend's house. My turn came so I stepped on and gave myself a little push. I didn't fall so I figured I was good. Wrong." He talked with his hands. They rolled and undulated as he spoke. We were shoulder to shoulder against the wall. He felt warm and solid next to me.

"I could roll but couldn't stop. I made the ramp jump—it was barely a foot off the ground—but I stayed on the board too long. I rolled down the six feet to the intersection as a car drove by. Hit me perfect. Fucked up my knee, broke this thigh bone." He slapped his thigh. "I lay there moaning and bleeding and crying for my mama until the paramedics came. I was seventeen."

Frank materialized in front of us.

"Work to do. You coming or are you flirting?"

James grinned at him. "She was just saying yes to dinner."

"Were you?"

I stood up carefully. "Do you need me?"

"I never need you. Enjoy your dinner." Frank nodded at James and walked away.

"Is he always so abrupt?"

"That's Frank," I said.

"So about dinner."

"No."

"Why not?"

"Because I'm busy."

"Too busy for dinner?" he said, smiling up at me.

"Too busy to be romanced. Dinner, movie, exciting conversation."

"Like movie dating," he said.

"Whatever. Yes."

"So what do you want?"

I looked up at this kid with his broad shoulders and earnest smile. I missed Simon so much. I missed his body. I wanted not to feel so alone. "Sex."

I left him standing there. Walked into the locker room and changed. When I came out James was in the ring sparring with a journeyman. Josef stood ringside watching James jab and dance around the ring.

I stood next to him and finally Josef noticed me. "You like?" he asked.

"Him? Don't know."

"He likes." He extended his hand and waved his thick fingers at me. Between his fingers a white business card. I took it. One side had James's name and a cell number; on the other side written in perfect penmanship, 1206 Westin.

"Thanks," I said and stowed the number in my jeans pocket.

I didn't go. At home his card went into my current bedside read. That night I slipped into blissful dreams with me starring as the boxer's girl.

11

The next night I met Frank at a bar he liked to frequent. The Mighty-Mighty was a dive bar that loved being one. Catering nearly exclusively to locals, crammed in among gray buildings at the tail-end of the downtown beautification project, it was a great place to get lost in and do business at. We weren't there ten minutes before James walked in.

"You gotta be kidding me," I said watching him cross the room toward me. He looked a little too fine in his gray suit.

"Eh, he's all right," Frank said. He drained the remainder of his beer.

"Excuse me? What do you mean he's all right?"

"I had a talk with him."

"Why?"

"Because you are an asset to Pritchard Investigations and we don't want to lose you."

"Simon put you up to this?"

"He wanted to make sure this guy wasn't interested in taking you away from us."

"Us?"

"Us," Frank said.

James made his way over as Frank pulled money out of his pocket. He dropped a ten on the table.

"Frank." James's smile was too big. They shook hands.

"See ya later, Cupcake," Frank said, then graciously offered his seat to James and left me to his set-up.

"May I sit?" James asked.

"Frank says you can."

He started to swing his ass in next to me but stopped himself. "But do you say I can?"

"Sure, but you're buying all the drinks."

"Done."

He sat and we talked about boxing. How he got in. How he's doing really. He was training for a big fight in six weeks in Reno. The payday was nice if he won but said he didn't really care about the money. He wanted to shut the other guy up. His opponent was a talker. "Talks trash all day, all night. I want to hurt him."

We ordered beers. He asked about my family.

"Brothers? Sisters?"

"No."

"A best friend then?"

"Yes, but she's dead."

That stopped him, drained away the playful banter. It stopped me too some days. I tried not to think of Fiona. I tried not to think about Simon. I tried not to think.

I asked if he had a best friend.

"My opponent—William Flynn," he said.

"So you don't talk anymore?" I said.

"We do. This fight's been coming for a long while now. He's annoying with his playing for the camera crap."

"So not mortal enemies."

"Sure we are. Right up until they ring the bell and declare the winner. Then we are friends again."

"That easy huh?"

"Why not? It's nothing personal. It's what I do. Not who I am." He held up his fists, studying them. "They say I could be great though." He sounded a little amazed.

"Do they?" I took a sip of my beer. My tone must have implied something because he's serious now.

"Yeah they do. Don't you know what I could do to you with these? You wouldn't stand a chance. Especially with the way you punched. You telegraph. If you fought like that in a real fight, you'd get hurt. You wouldn't stand a chance in a real fight."

Cocky asshole. "Do you know knives?"

"Like what kind?" He lowered his hands and took a long draw from his beer.

"Any knife. Any length, any size."

"You mean can I fight with one?"

"Yes."

"Probably. Sure."

"Good. Then you show up with your fists of fury there. And I'll show up with my knives and we see who wins that fight."

He blinked then a smile lit up his face. "I think I like you."

"Of course you do. I'm likeable."

I absolutely did not sleep with him. But I wanted to.

Before I left he offered to help me in the gym. He wanted to demonstrate the correct way to throw a punch. I declined. Frank seemed to take pride in teaching me. Or he liked seeing me fail on a regular basis. Either way, it would make Frank angry. I didn't need Frank angry.

12

The next day James called to invite me to dinner again. I let him buy me a drink instead. Back at the Mighty-Mighty I was four drinks in when I realized the prospect of a new man in my bed didn't phase me. There was enough alcohol in my system to make me think I could forget about Simon long enough to have a little fun.

He followed me to my place and I gave him the quick tour. Then I left him to peruse my bookshelves. I busied myself in my kitchen looking for the right glasses to pour tequila in while trying to figure out why I was having trouble breathing. I found two mismatched glasses, grabbed the bottle of tequila, steadied myself and walked out, determined to entertain my guest.

On my too small couch, he sat looking comfortable. He hadn't kissed me. Hadn't even tried yet. I handed him a glass and poured us each a shot's worth. I downed mine but he only held his.

"You okay?" he asked.

"Sure I am."

He leaned forward, set his glass on the floor and extended his hand to me. I took it and let him pull me down onto his lap. Our faces were inches apart. His long fingers worked their way beneath my shirt and rubbed the skin above the top of my jeans. The fingers were rough and sent little shocks through me.

He smelled like the gym—sweat, leather, and something else. Not unpleasant but the second he kissed me it all went sour. My breath caught and I pulled away, too far though. I teetered then fell off his lap and onto the floor.

"What?" James said reaching for me, touching my arm trying to guide me back to him.

"I can't," I shook my head. God, what am I doing? "I'm sorry," I mumbled, wiping my eyes. I was crying again. I'd done so much crying over these last few months, all the tears spilt over Simon. "There's someone else."

He nodded and dropped his hands. "There's always someone else."

I wanted James to be here. I wanted to be with him. "There wasn't supposed to be."

"So I'll go," he shook his head, stood up. "Should I even try to call you?"

"Persistent," I said looking up at him, feeling the heat of a blush on my face and the weight of Simon on me.

"Yes, I have to be. Besides I think you might be worth the fight. I like you." He leaned down a little, though it was obvious he was deliberately not touching me. He was close enough for me to feel the heat of his body and said, "And you like me."

He showed himself out. I stood up, surrounded by the walls that housed my memories of Simon and me. I heard James walking across my gravel driveway before I found my voice. I went to the door, called him back, "Don't leave yet."

"Are you sure?" he said once we were back in position, him on the couch and me on him. I kissed him a little rougher. He pushed me back to look at me.

"I want you here. It's just my head's in the way. It'll stop talking in a minute, give me a minute," I said and leaned in again, kissed him softly. I squeezed my eyes shut until I saw bright splashes of color. Until the impulse to pull away from him passed. I rode out the edge of fear and adrenaline until it didn't matter who I was kissing or whose hands were on me. Until want and need were all that drove me.

Later, while James slept and daylight was still hours away, Simon called.

"What are you doing?" he said.

"I'd ask you the same but I know her name."

"Oh, we're quick tonight."

"I have my moments. So what do you want?

"I have work for you."

"So tell Frank. Why call me?"

"Frank doesn't want to be our intermediary anymore. Said if I want you I should call you myself."

"Well, you've called."

"So do you have the time in between what you're doing?"

"Sure, he'll keep for a few days."

He filled me in. He spoke quickly, not bothering to charm me. James sighed something in his sleep. Simon hesitated. "Go on," I said, "he's still asleep."

"This guy, is he..."

"Do I ask you about her?"

"Don't screw up in New Mexico." He hung up.

It was a funny thing, the rush I got from ticking him off. I lay back down next to my boxer, confident that Simon wouldn't sleep nearly as well as I would.

When morning came, James was gone. He left me pancakes and a note written in his perfect penmanship.

13

I spent the next three days gone. A man in Tularosa, New Mexico needed to have a car accident. Setting it up was proving difficult. Frank's Zen-like calm in the face of adversity annoyed me.

"Waiting is an art, Cupcake. Learn it and you'll be that much closer."

"Closer to what?" We'd been sitting in a car for hours waiting and I was in no mood for a philosophy lesson.

"Closer to acceptable."

I knew all about waiting. I was still waiting for Simon to get a clue and realize that, hello, still the one. The right girl. The right everything for him. But letting those thoughts run around my mind would depress me. Besides I had James Vicario to look forward to when I got back so I was on vacation from my well-deserved pity party.

As full night descended on the city, our man showed up. He went down easy, in time for the flash flood warning to go out. It's tragic how many people never heed those flash flood warnings. He would be found days later, in his upside-down car, still belted in. Suspicious? Yes. But we got away clean.

***

Simon called me my first night back. "Frank has your money."

"Yep, I know."

"Come see me. I want to see you."

"Why?"

"I want to know you're all right."

"I'm fine."

"Laura."

"I have to go."

I couldn't hang up though. Neither could he. He missed me. I knew it, he knew it. We sat there listening to each other breathe for awhile.

***

I called James the next day and he spent the night. The day after he'd be in Reno and in two days he'd fight his friend. He was nervous and fidgeted so much he kept us both awake. The next morning his manager showed up to take him away.

"Good luck," I said.

"Don't need luck. Skill will win this fight." He scooped me off my feet and squeezed me tight.

"See you in a few days," I said.

James's manager called early the next morning. I heard:

Hospital

Coma

Bar fight

Please come.

I flew into Reno and called Frank on the way to the hospital.

"Find out what you can. I'll drive up," he said.

At the hospital, the manager was evasive. He wouldn't tell me exactly what happened, just the highlights. A bar fight. The bar was in the hotel. The men involved followed James out and shoved him into a waiting car. Beat the crap out of him: broken bones, lacerated liver. They dumped James blocks away, left him there bleeding.

Somehow I'd thought Simon had claimed all my tears, that I'd been pumped dry. But they ran unbidden down my face and onto James's hospital bed.

"Stay with him," Frank said after I had filled him in. He was still hours away. He made me swear I wouldn't leave the hospital. He'd look into things. "Stay with him. I'll call you back."

A day later James surfaced and the morphine let him smile at me without pain. I held onto the one undamaged hand. The doctors said that they would deal with the puzzle that was his left hand later when he was more stable. He would never box again.

He died the same day, while I slept awkwardly in a chair next to his bed. The blaring alarms jolted me awake. Nurses and doctors ran in. I was relegated to the edges. They worked in harmony, talked in jargon. Then he was gone. In the hallway, the doctor told us—the manager, the trainer and me, the boxer's girl—between the nerve damage and the morphine, that James didn't suffer.

***

That night Frank and I talked at the hotel where James had stayed. In the lobby he told me what he found out. The opponent's people offered James money to lose. Not uncommon but James refused. They offered him the prize money to lose. They wanted Flynn to be the next big thing. He still refused, laughed at them. He wouldn't go the easy route. He wanted to win. So they came after him the only other way they could.

Frank watched me. The ache was back. The dull soreness in my chest that throbbed in time with my beating heart. I couldn't do anything about Simon. I could do something now. "Where do we find them?" I asked.

"We don't. It's over."

I shook my head. "It's not over."

I felt a hand settle on my shoulder. I turned and looked up into Simon's brown eyes.

"Trust me. It is," Frank said.

Simon sat down next to me and Frank left.

"This isn't over," I said.

Simon stroked my cheek. "It has to be. Flynn isn't someone you can go after, Laura."

"He did this."

"Maybe but it's more likely his handlers decided to make a play."

"So I'm supposed to forget about this? Forget about James?"

"You can't even this score for him."

"Sure I can." I got up and headed for the front doors. Simon grabbed my arm pulling me toward the elevators. I'm not sure why I let him pull me into a waiting elevator or why I let him hug me close.

"Laura," Simon said, his lips close to my ear, "you can't touch Flynn and they can't touch you."

Months ago, I couldn't imagine a life with someone else. Now I was torn between wanting to get justice for James and wanting to stay in Simon's arms. The warm familiar place, his chest with his familiar scent. I stayed there. He pushed the button for a floor and the elevator jolted upward. He pulled me out of the elevator and walked me down the hallway. He let me go and I leaned up against the wall.

"I don't think your girlfriend would approve."

"You need some sleep."

"I don't want to sleep." I levered myself off the wall.

"You do and you will sleep tonight. Tomorrow you'll see things my way. You'll understand."

I laughed at him. It sounded off, strained to my own ears. He opened the doors and pulled me into the room.

"Get on the bed."

"No foreplay? You used to like it when I stripped for you. Liked it when I rubbed..." He put his hand over my mouth, a frown on his face.

"You don't mean this. This isn't what you want, Laura. So get in the bed, let me cover you up and I'll stay until you fall asleep."

I opened my mouth to speak but I didn't trust myself. He pushed me backwards and I crawled up onto the bed. I lay on one side and he folded half of the bedspread over me. Then he lay next to me, placed an arm around me and nestled his face down into my hair, his breath warm on my neck.

He was gone by daylight. I was home the next afternoon. Ever the dutiful employee.

Two days after James's funeral, Reno newspapers reported that a car accident killed two. The only survivor was William Flynn.

Frank told me later that Flynn didn't know about the bribe. Flynn swore that Jimmy was his best friend and he was sick over his death. Frank believed him. I didn't.

14

Simon called to tell me that my father was sitting in his office
and could I please come and collect him? So I did. I took the
long way though hoping my hands would stop shaking
before I got there, all the while thinking what if it's not him?
How could Simon be sure? He'd only seen my father once in
pictures during the visit to my mother's house back in the
days when our love was new. It had been his idea. We
showed up at my mother's house one bright Saturday
morning and stayed until Tuesday. She'd loved him on sight.
Simon, dressed in his nice suit with his charming ways. He
kissed her on both cheeks and hugged her until she squealed.
That first night the neighbors came over and in her tiny
kitchen Simon played dominoes with them while my mother
cooked a feast appropriate for the first man her daughter
ever brought home. I peeled potatoes and carrots until
Simon said, "I'm losing, baby. Bring me some luck." And I
slid onto his lap and played his tiles while he kissed my neck
and whispered the dirtiest things into my ear. I fell in love
with Simon in that kitchen, the last piece in my heart shifting
into place. I wondered where he was when he decided he
didn't love me anymore.

I arrived at the tall, black-windowed bank building where
Pritchard Investigations had its new office. A perk of
mingling with the "right people" Simon said. His new
girlfriend had connections with the influential. She was from
money. She was tall, and blonde and tanned and I am none

of those things. Thus far I've only seen her twice, once during her office tour when most of the office was still in boxes. She said hello to everyone but made a point of walking over to me and we just gazed at each other, smiles firmly in place. What was there to say? Later my former boyfriend, now just my boss said, "She likes you." It was all I could do not to reach over the desk and punch him. Now, standing in his office while he gave my father a rundown of my life in Vegas (the g-rated version that didn't include the killing I did for him), like this was a parent-teacher conference and I was his most gifted student, I had to resist the urge again.

My father looked uncomfortable in the office chair. He didn't look me in the eye. But I looked at him. I looked and looked at him, trying to see me in him. It had been nearly seventeen years since I saw him last. Nearly sixty now, his hair was still black, with the exception of a little gray around his ears. When he stood, claiming he was tired and he really just wanted to see me and thanks for the tour and it was a pleasure to meet you, he towered over Simon. I had forgotten just how big my father was. All these years I had only dreamed about his back, the sound his shoes had made on the wooden steps as he made his escape. I'd forgotten him as my father. Well, most of me had anyway but there was a small part, perhaps in my pinky toe, that housed what was left of the ten-year-old girl I had been. The girl who still adored this man, the girl who thought Joe Park was Superman.

I had to take him somewhere to talk but I wasn't bringing him to my house, I couldn't stand the idea of him in my home against the backdrop of my walls, and I wasn't going to his hotel room. So I decided to take him to Denny's. The one on Fremont near Eastern, where it's never busy and the staff would leave you alone. We slid into a booth seat and feigned interest in the menu before ordering coffee and I ordered a scoop of vanilla ice cream to pacify my ten-year-old self, to shut her up. She wanted to hug her father and cry and tell him how much she'd missed him. She wanted to know where he'd been. Was he staying? Would he and momma get back together? I let her ramble on while staring at him. My father. He tried a smile but it looked pained. He didn't know this version of me. I had spent the last three years becoming this version of me. A me who used Frank Joyce as role model for my transformation. And really, no one wants their daughter to grow up to be like Frank. Dear Daddy, Frank taught me how to kill today. Frank taught me how to fight, how to take a punch and get back up. How to make people fear me. How to give a punch that would bring a man to his knees and, once there, how to finish him off. Frank was my teacher, my partner, my guide. When I grow up I want to be just like Frank and not you.

The coffee and ice cream arrived and I loaded up a heap of melting vanilla and slid it into my mouth. I let the cold rest on my tongue just like when I was little. He laughed and I opened my eyes (when had they closed?).

"Nice to see some things stay the same," he said.

My mouth was too full to speak so I looked him over again. Mapped the wrinkles on his pale face. The lines around his eyes and mouth. We have the same eyes, colored a brown so dark as to be mistaken for black. Other than this loose connection, there was nothing physical that connected us. We could be strangers having coffee instead of a father and daughter. I blinked back tears and swallowed.

"I lied for you and kept lying to Fiona—my best friend—to protect you." Maybe to protect myself too. "How could I tell her that my father had killed hers? God, they cried so long."

Forever it seemed to my ten-year-old self. The last time I'd been home Fiona's mother was still crying, adjusting pictures of her family while she wiped at her face and told Simon all about her dead husband and dead daughter. She thought she was cursed, my mother had told me. "Tell me something. Why did you cry, Dad? Was it because he was begging you not to do it? To think of his girls—his wife, his daughter?"

My father rubbed his hands over his face. "I did think of them."

"You killed him and you left me. And Mom. You didn't think about us."

He slammed his hand on the table. He turned around searching for our waitress. On his neck were purplish blotches. He'd dyed his hair recently. Dyed his hair for me maybe.

He turned back and tears were in his eyes. "Jerry owed people money. Jerry always owed somebody money."

"You could have covered for him." My voice was so small. I wanted to stay angry but she wouldn't let me. The girl I was whispered about the time he took her fishing and all the times he re-read *Anne of Green Gables* to her.

"You think I hadn't? But Jerry, he was always looking out for the sure thing. A quick fix. I couldn't that time."

I knew the kind of man Jerry had become. I'd met men like him. The ones who owed so much money they decided to disappear rather than stay and lose their knees or their lives. Running was never the right answer and when they did run, they often found Frank and me waiting for them. I nodded to keep him talking.

"It was him or maybe his whole family. To send a message. They told me to do it or they'd send someone who wouldn't care if Fiona was there or, worse, they wouldn't stop at killing Jerry. Maybe the guy would pay his respects to Jerry's wife and daughter. Could I let that happen? You girls were supposed to be fucking asleep. His wife was supposed to be asleep. He wasn't supposed to cry. He wasn't supposed to beg." My father rubbed his face again and looked down at the table.

"The money they paid me was enough for your mother to move north like she wanted. Into the nicer suburbs. Why weren't you asleep?" His voice cracked on the last question. The sting of oncoming tears hurt my nose.

I told him the truth. Fiona and I had never gone to sleep. We'd stayed up late talking and reading from the book Fiona had taken from her mother's stash under the bed. Some romance book with a bare-chested Fabio and some windswept brunette on the cover. I could almost laugh at the silliness of it. I told him that I lost the deciding game of rock, paper, scissors so I was the one who had to sneak downstairs for cookies and milk. If I had picked scissors instead of rock, it would have been Fiona who heard him talking to her father. Heard her father crying. It would have been Fiona who crept close to the kitchen door and pushed it open just far enough to see her father tied to a chair. Fiona would have screamed. But I lost that night. It was me who watched my father run his hand over her father's head then step back and aim the .38. It was me who saw the way the gun trembled in his hand. It was me who pushed the door open wider and stepped in after the bullet had left the gun and ended the life of a man I had called Uncle.

"You made me swear I wouldn't tell Fiona. You made me pretend that I saw nothing," I said. "And then you left me."

"I know." He ran his finger in endless loops around the rim of his coffee cup. A minute went by then another. Then he said, "So you know, your mother made me leave."

I shrugged. "She made me leave too." He nodded at this piece of information. He knew my mother better and it couldn't be a stretch for him to imagine how tightly she hung on to me. How forcefully she boxed me into the form of her ideal daughter. The daughter with straight A's on her report card and exceptional parent-teacher conferences. The state college came calling on her perfect daughter, wanted her to attend. Examination scores like mine were few and you could be their poster child for public schools. I smiled like they wanted. Allowed my mother to steer my academic life. All the while Fiona and I were plotting our escape.

The waitress came over with the carafe and poured more coffee. She took away the melted puddle that was the vanilla ice cream. She smiled at my father a little too widely and swung her hips unnecessarily. My father watched her leave but he didn't really seem that interested.

"I thought you were married to Simon," he said. "Your mother seemed to think that you were marrying him."

"I never told her that," I said, too quickly. "We broke up a while back. He's with someone else." Someone blonde, someone appropriate.

"But you work for him?" His brow creased into long furrows of pale skin. "What do you do for him? You're not a licensed private investigator, are you?"

"No," I said.

"Then what?"

I should tell him the truth but Joe Park's little girl doesn't want her father to think less of her so a sliver of the truth will do. "I do what he asks of me."

"For money." This was more statement than question. I couldn't stop the smile that crept across my face.

"Yes." It all made sense now. He thought he knew something about me and my life here among the neon lights and endless rows of stucco houses. He wanted something.

I leaned back to give room to the other side of my ten-year-old self. The one that came to be after the blood was spilt and the lies were told.

"You're his whore."

I felt my jaw slacken. I sat still for a moment. I considered what he said. A whore. Was I Simon's whore? I shook my head and asked, "Is that what you were, Dad?"

I saw the slap coming but I didn't try to stop it. I took a breath and closed my eyes as the blow landed and split my lip.

"Hey," said the waitress. She wasn't smiling at him anymore. "You son-of-a-bitch, you stop that." She stalked over to us, ready to do something. But I put a hand up to stop her.

"It's okay. I'm fine." I smiled at her. The split lip was doing nothing to reassure her but she backed off.

To him I said, "Some family reunion." I licked my lip and tasted the blood there. "You took money. You accepted it as trade for Jerry's life."

"For Fiona and her mother," he said pointing his finger in my face. I could see now how the joints of his fingers were large and knobby. Arthritis probably. That slap probably hurt him more than it hurt me. Frank hit harder and with more affection.

"We're done now."

"You are better than this."

"I'm better than you, Dad. What do you want really?"

"I promised your mother."

Of course. I saw what I had missed earlier. He was wearing his wedding ring. I could hear my mother telling him to make peace with me and then he'd be back on her good side and into her house that's paid off. The house I paid off for her.

"You need money?" I said.

"No."

"A job?"

He looked away when he said, "I know what you do."

"Good, then you know where I learned it. You're a good teacher, Dad."

"They caught me, Laura. I did time for killing him."

"Good. You deserved it. Do you feel remorse? Do you feel at all?"

"Of course I do. But I did my time. It's behind me."

"Not for killing Jerry, Dad. For me. You ran away before they caught you. You sold out the people you worked for and left me behind." He turned his face to the window. The discussion was over. He was finished rehashing what he'd done wrong and so was I.

I paid the check. The waitress gave me my change and a plastic bag of ice. I thanked her and left as she began to tell me in a low whisper there were places I could go to get help. I got in my car and spent one final moment looking at him. Then I drove away.

15

Three steps into the backroom of the bar where Simon was having his bachelor party a man rose up from his position at the poker table and bellowed at me, "Finally, the entertainment is here."

I hesitated, glanced around at the other men at the table. One was Frank, to his right sat Simon and another man, dark hair, nice suit, had his back to me.

"Well, are you coming over here or what, baby?" said the man.

Frank was grinning a little too broadly. He probably won a bet on how fast I, playing the role of Little Miss Desperate, would get here after Simon's call. It took me three hours and an hour of that was the necessary priming.

Hope he lost.

"Sit down," Simon said to the man. He left his chair and we walked toward each other. There was appreciation in his green eyes as he gave me a slow once-over. I wore four-inch black heels and the barest slip of a dress. He raised an eyebrow like I was overdressed but I could tell he liked what he saw.

What was it about good-looking men? Simon was the walking, talking version of every bad habit I wanted to have. He was junk food and nicotine, heroin and cocaine. It'd been six months since he cut me loose to float balloon-like, abandoned and lost. I couldn't help hoping he'd re-inflate me.

"Hello, beautiful." He slid an arm around me and I felt myself rise at his touch. "Let's introduce you." He guided me over to the table. "Frank you know, of course." He gestured to the dark-haired man. "This is Oscar, an old friend of mine and the loud mouth is Buddy, Oscar's partner."

Buddy grinned and revealed a mouth full of braces. Oscar gave me a nod.

"She's the stripper, right?" Buddy's words were slurred and he was leaning a little. At first, I thought he was drunk but he was trying for a better look at my legs. I didn't like his mouth and the way his eyes raked over me.

"No, I'm here to kill you." I felt Simon's arm tighten around me.

"A comedian? Geez, Simon couldn't you get the old lady to okay a stripper?" Buddy said.

The old lady? I liked that description of the soon-to-be Mrs. Simon Pritchard. Perhaps I judged Buddy too quickly. He winked at me, crunching ice from his drink and spraying the table.

Never mind.

Simon patted my ass and settled me into the other open chair nestled between Buddy and Oscar. "Buddy, this is Laura. Be nice to her and she may be nice to you." Simon tossed me a wink as he took his seat again. Frank smirked and I wished I'd never left Vegas.

"Gonna play?" Frank asked, shuffling the cards.

"Yes, she's playing. Deal her in. I'll cover her," Simon said. "Take Buddy's money will you? He's cleaning me out."

Buddy laughed as if something was stuck in his throat. I leaned away, moving an inch closer to Oscar. Five hands later, Buddy was the short stack and growling at his drink.

"This is complete shit. You called in this fucking ringer with her tits hanging out and expect any of us to play well?" He sucked down the last of his drink and crunched more ice.

I had to agree, this was complete shit. Here I was playing poker at my ex-boyfriend's bachelor party. He was getting married tomorrow. The day after that he'd be on some beach and I'd be watching some husband or wife doing something they shouldn't. Depending on the client, I'd either take pictures or kill them.

Love sucked.

Another few hands and I'd given back a large chunk of my winnings. Simon winked at me and I was struck again by just how stupid this was. Screaming seemed crazy but it was all I wanted to do.

"Bathroom?" I asked.

Frank jerked his head towards the door I came in. I grabbed my purse and went to the restrooms. Between the two matching doors was an upholstered bench. I sat down, arranged my skirt so I wouldn't stick to the pleather, leaned my head back and closed my eyes. Kicking myself was easier this way.

I made out their distant laughter above the sounds of electronic poker. A low rumble from Frank and Buddy's trying-too-hard laugh. Nothing from Oscar. It was two a.m. and I needed a drink.

I was foolish enough to think he actually wanted me. His phone call held such promise: "Come down here. I'd love to see you tonight." And with that, I shaved and curled, lacquered and primped myself from head to toe and then drove two hours to arrive at this roadside bar and be mistaken for a stripper.

I heard footsteps and the quick scuff of shoe as someone stopped abruptly. I opened my eyes to see Simon leaning against the wall next to the men's room.

"Oh, look. It's the bridegroom."

"Are you okay?"

That goddamn question. For months, I ducked around that question and the pitying looks that accompanied it. Maybellyne gave me her poor-you face every time I came into the office. Frank allowed my boxing lessons to deteriorate into angry shoving matches. I usually ended up crying on a mat but it wasn't because of too many body shots from him.

"I'm at a bachelor party for my ex. I'm perfect." For the first time since we met, I wished Simon would leave me alone.

He exhaled loudly. "Come here, I want to talk to you."

"Fuck you. We've talked plenty. I'm going home." I got up to leave but he grabbed me, yanked me towards him. I teetered dangerously and had to lean into him or fall. That touch sent me delving into memories of us. I knew every twitch of each muscle on this man. It was too much. "Simon, let go." I hated sounding weak. I hated being weak for him. I hated him. I missed him.

I felt his warm breath on my cheek and then he pushed me through to the men's room. The smells of old urine and stale floral scent from long-dead air-fresheners wrapped around my nose. I tried not to breathe. Then Simon didn't give me another chance to try. He pushed me back against the door and leaned his body hard into mine, kissing me with a force that I understood. He was a little desperate too. The door's hydraulics fought against us, unwilling to close any faster than its design.

"You look fucking amazing." His hands latch onto me at eight and two, his left on my ass and his right on my breast. I squeaked in response to the pain. The pain was familiar and good. The pain was clarity.

He wanted me. Not her. In that moment, with his teeth on my neck and my hands unbuckling and unzipping his pants, we were again what we had been:

Together.

Happy.

Insatiably horny.

The door was pushed from the outside. Simon ripped his mouth away from mine to curse at the person on the other side. He pulled me away and shoved me against the counter. Then he positioned me between the dual sinks and I felt the biting cold of the tiled counter on my ass. His hands under my skirt, he yanked my panties off. He pulled me closer still and slid home. He leaned his chest into me, over me and my head met the mirror. I banged my head and tailbone with each stroke. It was so good I couldn't stop the tears that flowed. He slowed a moment to lick them away then we picked up the pace again and we were anywhere but in a men's bathroom at a dive bar in the desert.

Breathing hard, collapsed on top of me, he rested his forehead against mine. "I can't believe I have to give you up."

If I'd had a voice, I'd have told him he didn't have to. I'd have told him not to marry her. Told him anything he wanted to hear if it meant still being with him, even in a bathroom. But my throat was sore and my voice felt out of reach. I shook my head and stroked his face.

"Do something for me." He kissed me again, an endearing bottom lip-nibbling kiss He stowed himself away and zipped up. His brown hair was rumpled and his tie was askew. I lifted my hand to smooth his hair but he moved just out of reach.

"Buddy needs a ride back to Vegas. Give him a lift, but leave him in the desert. Standard pay out." He caressed my thigh and then was gone before I could formulate an answer.

Of course, Simon "All Business" Pritchard called me to do a job. I guess I should have felt lucky to have gotten the fuck from him. I felt the cold from the counter again. I turned to look at my reflection but the water-spotted mirror only showed my eyes, raw and sad. Well, ain't that me all over. Fuck.

16

I remained where Simon dumped me for so long I wasn't surprised when the door opened. Oscar took two steps in and stopped. He looked me over, from heels to naked ass on counter to tear-streaked face.

"Damn, woman. You okay?"

Fuck me. That question again.

"Go away." I didn't try to cover up. I wasn't going to give him the satisfaction of seeing me embarrassed.

"Want some help down?" He took a step closer.

"Any closer and it's gonna be you who needs help."

At this, he smirked. Then he left me to my misery. As soon as the door closed, I peeled my ass off the counter, returned my panties to their proper position and retrieved my purse from the floor. I cleaned myself up and thought I qualified as presentable when the door opened again. Frank stepped in. He glanced my way but didn't stop. He lined up at the urinal. I waited. I heard him zip up and flush. I knew Frank. He'd have something to say. He'd been waiting for hours, maybe months to say it. He stood next to me and washed his hands. I pulled paper towels from the dispenser and handed them over.

"I gave Buddy a little something. He has a habit. He shouldn't be too much trouble."

"Great," I said. Scenarios for Buddy's disposal ran through my head.

He threw his paper towels away. "So, you gonna need some help with him?"

I glared at him. "You don't think I can take care of him?"

"I only meant that you don't exactly look like you're dressed for digging a hole tonight," he said.

I backed down. He was right. He's always right. "Yeah, I guess I could use the help. Got a shovel?"

"Never leave home without it. What did you bring to the party?"

"My cleavage." I said.

"You win." He pulled me into a bear hug. His familiar scent of aftershave, cigar and sweat overpowered the bathroom smells and I breathed in deep.

***

My extended bathroom stay allowed me to miss Simon and Oscar's departure. Buddy was high and sleepy. He stood, eyes closed, leaning against the door. His head dipped forward as sleep tried to claim him. I turned my smile on high and slipped between tables, cooing Buddy's name. He jerked awake and nearly fell, but he recovered.

"Hello, Brown Sugar." He drooled across my ear as he pulled me in for a hug. I pushed away and tried to dodge an alcohol-soaked kiss but he kissed me wet and sloppy. I was terrified my lip was going to get caught in his grillwork. He released me relatively unharmed but I had to rein in the impulse to go brush my teeth.

"Ready to go?" I asked.

"Sure thing, baby. Show me the way." He leaned heavily on me. Frank took up my other side and the three of us wedged ourselves through the door and to my truck.

Frank pulled Buddy off me and helped him into the cab of my truck. Buddy peered blearily at us, arranged himself against the truck's door and slept. Past his bedtime, indeed.

"Where are we going?"

"Just follow," Frank said, brushing past me and squeezing his bulk into his own car. I followed him out onto the two-lane black-top road. Twenty minutes later, under the jet-black sky, Frank pulled over and I did the same.

Frank walked around to Buddy's side. I heard the clank of metal hitting metal, the shovel meeting the truck bed with force. He opened the door and pushed Buddy over closer to me. His head lolled and he snored a little.

"Drive out there, Cupcake. Let's go explore the desert." He pointed out into the blackness to our right. We headed out slowly, headlights cutting through the dark ahead of us until Frank said, "Here."

He got out and Buddy snored on softly. Frank dropped the tailgate and the shovel shrieked across the truck bed. Buddy's eyelids fluttered but he settled back in, head tipped back. I got out. Frank met me at my door and pressed a gun into my hand. I opened my mouth to protest but he put a hand up to silence me.

"You, in those shoes and that short-ass dress, are not menacing. If I'm digging, you're Buddy-sitting."

I sat back behind the steering wheel and looked out into the darkness that surrounded us. Frank walked out and began to dig ten feet from where we parked. He grunted in time with Buddy's snores and I wondered where Simon was. Still driving or maybe at some private airport already on the plane getting ready to take off. All of our time together and this was how we end. Me in the desert and him in the clouds.

I look over at my charge. Close up, Buddy wasn't bad looking. With his face slack with sleep, he's almost handsome. I don't see a ring on his finger but what does that mean? I was as faithful as any wife should be, Buddy could be the perfect guy for someone. Not likely considering the people he ran with.

Twenty minutes in, Frank walked back over to us. He was panting a little, sweating a lot.

"Wake him up."

"Why? He isn't gonna be much use to you."

"I'm digging why should he be comfortable. Why should you? Get out." Frank walked around through the headlight beams and over to the other door. He yanked it open and grabbed a fistful of Buddy's shirt and suit jacket. Frank heaved him up and out, let him fall to the ground. "Wakey, wakey," Frank said as he dragged him in front of the truck's lights.

I got out and moved around to Buddy's side and crouched down. He was blinded by the lights and bewildered. Alcohol and whatever drug Frank had given him worked in tandem against his mind.

"What's going on?" Buddy squinted at me.

Slowly, wanting him to keep up with events, I said, "Buddy we're gonna bury you in the desert."

"What?"

"Yeah, sorry." Surprisingly, I was.

"You bitch."

So much for pity. I cracked Buddy on the forehead with the butt of the gun. He fell over whining and cradling his head. I stood up and backed away from him. "Not my fault you pissed off your partner."

"Oscar did this?" he asked, rubbing his head.

I shrugged. "I don't see him asking me not to kill you."

"What's he paying you? I'll pay you more."

"Sorry. Simon runs the show." I was just the entertainment. My feet hurt and dirt had worked its way between my toes. High-heeled sandals and the desert, not the best match. A dull throb emanated from my tailbone. Another bruise to remember Simon with.

I was close to shooting Buddy, getting in the car and driving back to Vegas. I bounced the gun in my hand a little, letting its weight fall back into my palm. I wasn't big on guns. I never used them. A knife was a quiet weapon. Sure, you had to get close but sometimes all you needed was a short skirt and a smile to get in close enough. But I was tired now and making an effort for Buddy didn't interest me.

He watched me. On his knees now, he said, "Look, let me talk to Oscar. He'll call it off. Let me talk to him or Simon."

"No coverage. Middle of the desert."

"Let me try." Buddy fumbled in his pockets and came up with a little black cell phone. The screen lit up when he opened it. Then he showed it to me, victorious. "Coverage."

I snatched the phone from his hand and he yelled, made a move as if he was coming after me. I raised the gun.

"Okay, okay." He sat back on the ground and hung his head. If he was thinking about how to get out of this, there was no evidence of it on his face. He only looked sad.

"How long did you work with Oscar?"

"Three fucking years. We made money, lots of fucking money. Real estate here and in Vegas. Legit money."

"So why does he want you dead?" This was a mistake. I knew it. This went against Frank's rules. Ten feet away, Frank heaved hard earth and grunted as he worked. He'd beat me senseless if he knew.

Rule Number Whatever—never ask questions. Do the job. It doesn't matter why. All that matters is that the job gets done and you aren't caught in the process. Do the job.

"Now that the market's gone south, he's started making deals without me. He's made some money on his own. Now he thinks he doesn't need me. It's business, I guess." He looked up at me then, tears balanced on the edge, ready to fall. "Are you really going to kill me?"

I flinched. I should've shot him. But no, I was gonna call Simon, more for me than for Buddy. Why not? I wanted to know why I'd been dumped. The underlying reason, the excuse that made the world tilt back and spin like it was supposed to. I'd been shaky ever since Simon let me go. I deserved a real reason, not the I've-met-somebody-else excuse he'd sent me.

"Okay, I'll call him."

Simon picked up on the third ring. "Hello." His tone was flat. I didn't hear anything. No laughing girls or sounds of the road.

"It's me," I said.

"Laura." His voice warmed up and with that alone, my name rolling gently out of his mouth, I forgave him. I leaned against the truck, felt the dull ache in my tailbone and drew in a long breath.

"Hey," I said.

"I can still smell you on me." The things his voice did to me. I picked up the edge of my dress and inhaled. He was there. His aftershave and sweat. Right there, on me. I closed my eyes and laughed

Buddy pulled me out of my reverie with his panicked, "Well?"

"Who's that?" Simon asked. "You're done, right?"

"Not exactly. He wants to talk to you."

"Fuck, Laura what are you doing?" The smooth heat in his voice receded and the flatness returned.

"Entertaining myself, I suppose."

"Where's Frank?"

"Digging a hole."

"Put him on." I figured he meant Frank. I gave the phone to Buddy instead. I turned away, parked myself behind the steering wheel and watched Buddy try to multitask walking and begging. He was stumbling.

Frank, finished with the hole, tossed the shovel back into the truck. He stood next to me, leaning on the door. We watched Buddy as he paced back and forth yelling into the phone.

"What's going on?"

"He asked to talk to Simon so I called him." I didn't look at Frank. He made a noise, something close to a growl. I looked. Frank's face was twisted and I readied myself for the swinging or the yelling. Neither came. His face relaxed.

"You wanna tell me why?"

"I was being nice. Last wish and all."

"Ha."

Frank's distaste for my attachment to Simon was palpable. Understandable. Frank's long-term relationships: his mother and me, his sidekick/punching bag in heels. We'd been together not quite a year now. Simon and I were together nearly two.

We turned our attention back to Buddy. He appeared to be listening now.

"Look, Laura," Frank began. Here it comes. The lecture. "You're gonna find somebody else. Somebody better than Simon."

I stared at him. "What if I don't?"

"You will." Frank jerked his gaze away from me. "Shit. Move over." Frank shoved me farther into the truck's cab and jumped in. I turned back to Buddy, but Buddy wasn't there.

Damn.

Frank gunned the motor and for a moment we didn't see him, then we did. Running to our right like a jackrabbit from a coyote.

"Little fucker," Frank said.

"Get alongside him." I pulled my seatbelt tight. We edged closer to the running man. Buddy ran, all knees and elbows, further into the desert. I rolled the window down.

"Hey, Buddy. Where ya going?"

He glanced over at me, eyes wide. He was still clutching the cell phone. "Let. Me. Go." The effort of speaking seemed to take the last of his energy. He slowed down but still he angled away from us. Frank stopped the truck, letting Buddy run unchallenged for a few seconds. Frank was deciding how best to end this.

"No, not that way." I knew Frank well enough to know that he wanted to run him down. The way his knuckles went white as his grip tightened on the wheel. The truck lurched into gear. We caught up to Buddy and right as the truck began to pass him, I opened my door, catching him full in the back with it. There was a loud thud and Buddy went down. The truck's right side lifted higher for a moment as we went up and over Buddy. I glared at Frank.

"What?" Frank turned the car and circled back to the point of impact.

"It's not your truck with blood and whatnot underneath now."

"Shut up and check him." He rammed the truck into park and we got out. In the twin beams of light, we saw Buddy stretched out before us, not moving.

"Do you see these shoes? I am not carrying him. I can't believe you ran him over," I said.

"We wouldn't be in this position if you hadn't decided to be nice."

"I didn't think he'd run, Frank. Where was he gonna go?" I said, gesturing to the great dark outdoors.

"All right, all right." He waved me off. "But I'm not digging another fucking hole."

Frank pulled the tailgate down and we stood over Buddy. His leg was broken. Blood streaked across his face. He was dead. In his hand, the phone was still in one piece. I pulled it free from his grasp, wiped the blood off on his suit jacket and read the display. The call was still active.

"Hello," I said.

"What happened?" Simon said.

Frank walked around the body then bent down to lift him. I turned away and walked a few feet into the darkness.

"He's dead," I said.

"He ran." I pictured Simon running a hand through his hair. Classic I'm-disappointed–in-you fashion.

"Yeah."

"About tonight…"

There was no point to Simon and I talking. Talking to him made the knot in my chest twist painfully. "It's fine. I get it."

"Get what?"

"What I mean to you. I understand now. I didn't before but now I do. It's business."

A pause then he said, "Yeah, it is."

"But you still want me." His silence was all the answer I needed. "Have a nice wedding." I hung up.

With Buddy in the truck's bed we drove back to the hole and I helped Frank drag Buddy to his new resting place. We covered him up, then we got back in the truck and Frank drove us back to the main road and his car.

At his car, he threw the truck into park and made sure to slam the door to punctuate his exit. I slid over and watched him stomp to his car. I thought he was going to go and I was all ready imagining my next boxing lesson with him. The body blows I'd have to take to make up for my behavior tonight. Then he walked back.

"Next time, keep your personal shit out of this. Do you understand?" He stabbed a meaty finger in the air in front of my face.

"I know. I'm sorry. This is business." Truly sorry for tonight.

"That's right." He reached out and punched my shoulder lightly. "Let's go home."

17

I shouldn't have called in. That was my first mistake. My second was walking into the hotel's parking garage while yapping away to Frank on the phone. Listening to Frank tell me that Simon had called to say that he and his new bride would be taking a few extra honeymoon days had me so aggravated I was nearly in tears.

"Did he ask about me?"

"No."

"Great. Just great." I weaved blindly down the aisle to my rental. I didn't look anywhere but ahead of me.

"Do the job and come home."

"Yeah, okay, but Frank," I didn't get to finish the sentence. I was slammed into the side of my car then grabbed by the throat and hoisted up off my feet. My head collided once, twice, against the concrete wall of the garage and the plastic clip that held my hair in place exploded into pieces.

"You take her fucking money and you go shopping?" said the man as he squeezed my throat tighter. I kicked and twisted but he just slammed me again. He pressed his body against mine to hold me still. Distantly, I could hear Frank calling my name repeatedly.

My vision blurred. I was going down fast. I swung at his face with one hand and clawed desperately at my belt with the other. The guy grabbed my hand as it came toward his face, pinned it against the wall.

"How could you do that? She came to you for fucking help." His voice was low but the anger in it scared me more than anything. He was going to kill me. My fingers closed on the hilt of the small knife hidden behind my belt buckle. I palmed it and while he leaned into me, anger coming off him like summer heat off pavement, I pressed the blade to his throat. He froze and I hung there.

"Let. Go." I rasped out with the little breath I had. He didn't move. I pressed the blade harder into his throat. I heard him suck in a breath, then I was falling. I landed on my feet and fell over onto the car's hood. With each breath, my vision cleared and I could see my assailant better. He'd retreated to the end of the stall. He was six foot tall, pale, and angry. He wiped at his throat, looked at the blood on his hand. I leaned down and found the phone.

"Bitch," he said.

"Fucker," I put the phone to my ear. "Frank, you there?"

"What the hell." He sounded relieved.

"I'm gonna have to call you back."

"Wait," he began but I ended the call.

"She paid you to do a job."

She. The client. Forty-eight hours ago I sat across from the mother of a dead twenty-five-year-old man while she explained to me how her son died. A hit-and-run supposedly. But she had found out through a friend that the son's wife had paid someone to kill him. Now Eileen—fifty, nice, suburban, distraught—wanted a little payback. Whatever it took.

"I'm doing the job asshole. Who the fuck are you?" I rubbed my neck. I could feel the points of contact on my neck like a brand. Oh yeah, it was gonna bruise.

"I sent her to you."

So this was the friend. The friend who had told her about her daughter-in-law and then helped her find me by way of Frank, my associate, my teacher, my almost-friend.

"I followed you. Every step you've made. You've done nothing."

"Nothing? So you followed me to her home last night? You saw what I saw when she left out her back door?"

Footsteps came toward us and we looked over to see a man looking concerned. "Everything okay, miss?"

I looked at Eileen's friend in his neutral corner. "Yeah, I'm fine. Thanks." I gave him a little smile. He looked at the two of us again then moved off.

"Do you wanna finish this somewhere else or should I just expect you to attack me again at some later date?"

"Fine. I won't touch you again."

"You're damn right. Room two oh five. Ten minutes."

He backed away and gave me a clear path to the elevator. I pushed the second-floor button and leaned against the wall. Fuck.

***

I reached my floor and slowly made my way down the hallway. In my room, I collapsed on the loveseat that faced the door. I was jittery. The rush of adrenaline was subsiding. I breathed deep and slow. I needed to call Frank.

"What the fuck?" Frank said.

"I guess someone else is in on this job. A friend of our client, I think. I'll talk to him."

"Get out now."

"No, it's fine. I've got this under control."

"Laura. You don't have shit under control. I never should have let you fucking go."

"You can't babysit me forever, Frank. I'm handling this. I'll call." I hung up. Garage Guy would be here any minute and arguing with Frank could take all night. I opened the door and let it rest just a little open. My knife in hand, I waited for his footsteps. A minute later, I heard him. He hesitated before knocking.

"It's open," I said. I leaned back on the couch and crossed my legs. Cool and casual. The door pushed open fractionally, then all the way. He stood in the doorway looking at me over the upholstered chairs. "Have a seat."

He moved slowly checking the room. Doing what I should have done in the garage. Frank was gonna have my head for fucking this up. I was careless.

"Do you have a name?"

He sat on the edge of the chair and leaned forward. "Cleveland Tully."

He was thirty, maybe a little older. A little gray at his temples. A general hard look that expressed some knowledge that life sucks. I could relate.

I picked up the cell phone and called my client. I figured she'd answer within three rings. She was waiting to hear from me. Waiting to get the call that she had gotten her money's worth.

"Hello?" There was a quaver to her voice and I pictured the gaunt woman who had asked me to kill for her.

"It's not done yet, Eileen. Sorry to call but do you know a Cleveland Tully?"

She gasped. "He's there?"

"Describe him." She did, right down to his dark, brown eyes. "He's here." She asked to speak to him and I offered the phone to him. "She'd like a word." He snatched it from my hand and walked over to the windows behind the couch.

"Hey, Eileen." Even from ten feet I could hear her giving him her opinion. He just stood there, nodding as if she could see him. Finally, he said, "I just wanted to make sure." He walked back to me and gave me the phone. All of the anger seemed to have drained away. He returned to his seat.

I put the phone to my ear said, "Any more surprises?"

"No and I'm very sorry. I hope...I hope you'll still do what I asked."

"Unless I run into more trouble, you'll hear from me when it's done." We said our goodbyes and I hung up. He looked uncomfortable now. I noticed his neck was still bleeding. I went into the bathroom, wet a washcloth and brought it and two hand towels out with me. I handed him the wet washcloth and one dry towel; got ice from the freezer section in the little refrigerator and laid it, wrapped in the other towel, on my neck. I watched him undo his coat and pull off his cap. Long brown curls unfurled crowding in at all corners of his face. In that moment, he lost years. I put him closer to thirty now. He dabbed at his neck.

"Cleveland, huh? Why did your parents do that to you?"

"My mom missed Ohio."

"I guess it could've been worse."

"Yeah, my dad was from Boise." He almost smiled, then reconsidered. "You didn't leave the hotel last night."

"How would you know?"

"Your car never left."

"This is Portland. Scenic views, mountains, public transportation. Walking is encouraged."

"You walked?"

"Why not? Lonnie did and I followed her. She left out her back door about midnight. Walked for about a mile, met a guy in a tow truck. Got in and they left. Guess he was the new boyfriend. Truck had JG Auto & Towing stenciled on the side. But I bet you knew that already because you followed me, right?"

He grumbled something.

"Sorry I didn't catch that."

"I've been trying to find the guy for a week, you're here a day and you've found him," he said.

"You're not too bad. You're the one that convinced Eileen her son was murdered by his wife, right?"

"She knew he was. I just happened to hear some crucial details before I got out."

"Got out?"

He didn't look me in the eye when he said, "Prison, up until two weeks ago. I got into a fight in a bar with guy. He died. It was an accident. I went to jail."

I nodded. Who was I to judge?

"Anyway," he continued, "another guy was talking about his cousin getting a sweet five-k payday. I didn't think

88

anything of it but then I hear this cousin offed some wife's husband and he was still banging her."

"And you put two and two together and got your murdered friend? That's a reach isn't it? And you told Eileen?"

"She deserved to know. It wasn't a stretch to me. I was supposed to hear that conversation. I was meant to see the connections. It was fate."

"Fate?" I laughed.

"You don't have to believe in it."

"It's not that, Mr. Tully I just expected to hear about God, not fate."

"Why God?"

"I didn't mean to insult you. You tell me you've just got out of prison. Far as I know, your options are to go to school, find God or join a gang."

"Shows what you know about prison."

I shrugged. "So you get out and tell Eileen her daughter-in-law killed her son. What do you gain?"

"I need to gain something?"

Frank's voice echoed in my head. He loved to offer up random tidbits of conversational wisdom when I was sore and panting on his boxing ring floor.

"There is always an angle, Cupcake. You don't see it you're gonna be fucked."

"Yes," I said, "so what do you gain?"

He squinted at me as if he knew something about me. "How old are you anyway?"

"Old enough. Why? Think you need an old man, arthritic with experience. Some Obi-Wan who can feel the force and kill with just a raised hand?"

A smile. "No, you just look young."

"I'm twenty-seven."

"For ten years, Tom wrote me a letter a week. He was just some kid who got in some trouble at fifteen and they put in this program to set borderline kids on the right track. It got cancelled after a year but he still wrote to me. We got to be good friends. He told me about meeting her, Lonnie. Hell, he even asked my advice on how to propose." He laughed a little. "What did I know? I was barely twenty when I went in, but he needed my opinion, my approval maybe. I don't know. But I mattered to him. I counted. My own family, one visit a year and even that stopped after a while. Tom was a good guy. That woman killed my friend."

He took a breath. "Have you ever lost someone? They said he died on the pavement. Breathing out his last breaths with no one around." Tully leaned forward and his whole face seemed to pull down. His eyes searched my face. He wanted to see some comprehension. Some understanding. I understood more than I wanted to admit to this stranger.

"I lost someone."

"What happened?"

Poor Fiona. Beautiful, addicted and dead before I could save her. "Someone helped her to an early grave."

"What did you do?"

"I returned the favor." Jimmy Mac died on an isolated road between Vegas and the brothel he liked to visit. He was my first kill. Sometimes I think I keep trying to get that feeling back. The feeling of complete satisfaction that washed over me when he died knowing that it was me that outplayed his Irish ass. "Tell me. You're young, strong," I fingered my neck. "Why am I doing this and not you?"

"She doesn't want me back in jail. Tom wouldn't want me to do more time because of him so she doesn't either. She's a nice lady."

"She is."

"So you understand then."

"I do."

"I want to be there. I want to see her dead. She's never met me. She wouldn't know me at all."

I shook my head. "Give me your number. I'll call you and Eileen when it's done." He opened his mouth as if to argue but then changed his mind and gave me his number.

He said, "Don't fuck this up."

"Just don't get in my way."
He left. No goodbyes.

18

The last twenty-four hours I had spent shopping just as Cleveland said. I found adorable boots with a good solid heel I could run in if necessary, a very nice butcher's knife from a kitchen store and the smaller knife I had used on him had come from a hunting store.

I visited the library and found through archived neighborhood newsletters that local booster clubs came by to drop off dinners during these painful months for Lonnie Franklin, the grieving widow. Local papers briefly speculated that she may have played a role in her husband Tom's death but she had an alibi. The life insurance policy paid out two hundred thousand. Pictures of the woman just before and right after the funeral still showed a vibrant woman. The woman I watched as she got her mail and walk her dog was a pitiful sight. No makeup, three-inch roots and sad-looking sweats.

Later, I drove the route to the bar where Cleveland believed Lonnie would meet and pay the man who killed his friend. At eight o'clock, Lonnie Conklin left her house in her car looking like a new penny. A drugstore-dye job and frizzy ends, tube top and too-tight jeans finished the transformation from faithful widow into cheap date.

I followed in my rental keeping her in sight until I was sure where she was headed then I fell behind and let her drive out of sight.

I'd give her a half hour to settle in and have a drink. I wanted to see if the boyfriend was here already and to see if Cleveland would make an appearance too. I nearly called in to the office. Just to see if Simon had returned yet. I couldn't bear the thought. I didn't really want to hear his voice again. Less than a week ago, I had nearly told him I loved him, now he was married and I was here in Portland. I didn't call.

***

There were a dozen people in the bar. Some around the TV and more around three pool tables that lined the middle of the room with a fourth table next to an exit. Most were in their twenties, though a few looked like hard-drinking regulars. The regulars were on stools at the bar itself and there alongside them was Lonnie Franklin.

She swayed gently to the Top Forty emanating from the jukebox and chewed on a stirrer. I sat down a stool away and ordered a margarita on the rocks. She smiled at me, looked left then right and then leaned over.

"Are you here alone?"

"Yeah."

"Me too. I haven't been out in ages." She straightened back up and bounced on her seat.

Frank had taught me many things during our time together. A code of sorts, rules to kill by. Never lie unless you have to. It's easier to keep up with the truth.

"It's been a while for me too. Recently dumped." I raised my margarita, toasted the air, and took a long drink. Good and cold. Heavy on the tequila. I thanked the bartender.

"You got dumped?"

"Yeah. It happens, right?"

"But you're so cute. Such a sweet face."

I had to smile. It's nice to commiserate a little. Share the misery of Simon.

"Thanks, but he found himself a tall blonde to hang himself with. Married her too."

Her mouth formed the perfect disbelieving 'O', pale pink lipstick glittering in the light of the neon bar signs. She shut her mouth, slapped the bar top and said, "Hey Sweet Cheeks, two more drinks." To me she said, "My husband died a few months back. I kinda miss him, ya know? But the best remedy for one guy is another. Now you drink that and the one that's comin' and here's to the new guy." She was hard not to like, even with her clothes ten years too young for her. An hour later, we had moved from the bar to the pool tables. She was breast to chest with some college junior who didn't know better. He was teaching her how to play pool. She dipped, giggled and flirted admirably.

She sauntered over swaying in her stilettos. "Come say hello to the cutie."

"Nah you go. He's a little young for me."

"You don't have to take him home, honey. Just pass the time with him." She pouted. Then her eyes shifted from my face to a point behind me and she stiffened. I turned to look. Approaching was a decent-looking guy. Bald, goateed and wearing a JG Autos work shirt. The patch on his chest said Elton.

"Know him?"

"Uh huh." She was twitching, her smile frozen on her face. Elton hugged her. Picking her up so her little high-heeled feet dangled.

"Hey Lonnie," he said.

"Hey," she giggled, hugging him to her. Over her head, Elton gave me a once-over and winked.

"A friend of yours?" he asked.

"Oh, this is Laura."

"Nice to meet you Laura." he grinned at me and took my proffered hand into his, covering mine. The hands were too warm, a little clammy. It was intimate. Too intimate. I pulled my hand back.

"Did you remember to bring it?" he asked Lonnie.

"Oh, um, yeah." Her wide-eyed gaze bounced from his face to mine then back again.

"Good." Elton turned away from us and called out to another couple across from us. "Hey man, play a game? Me and my girl against you and yours."

I went for beers and came back to find Elton putting money on the next shot. A hustler. Lonnie would be the one to turn over a rock and find a guy like him. I shook my head and watched Elton wring this guy dry then line up his next victim.

Elton played well. He made himself likeable. He was polite and agreeable. Bought them beers. After the last beer run, Lonnie came over.

"He's good," I said.

"Yeah." Lonnie grinned madly at me then leaned in close. "Looks like I'm not the only one getting some looks." She tilted her head, "There's a guy in the corner. You might think he's cute and he hasn't taken his eyes off of you."

I turned slowly to look the direction she'd indicated. Cleveland Tully, one hand on his drink, the other propping open a book in front him. Lonnie waved and Cleveland lifted his glass. I turned away.

"What do you think?" Lonnie bounced in place, tube top slipping. "Go talk to him." She yanked the blue top back into position.

"Don't think so." I hopped back up on the barstool and turned my attention back to Elton and the other pool players.

"Fine," Lonnie said and she went, off towards the bar. I should have seen this coming. Lonnie returned minutes later with a new friend in tow.

"Laura, this is Bob."

I turned to see Cleveland up close and personal. He looked good. The hard edge was still there but I could see the effort he was making to look relaxed.

He extended his hand, "Hi."

"Hey."

"Here, take my seat." Lonnie patted the other stool then all but skipped away to Elton's side. I just looked at Cleveland then shook my head.

"What are you doing here?" I said low. Back in this corner, we were far enough away from the random eavesdropper but still I kept my voice low and Lonnie in my sight.

"I was just waiting to see if she'd show."

I rolled my eyes. "I told you I'd call."

"All this waiting. I got impatient. Thought it wouldn't matter."

"And now you're sitting across from me in a bar like we're on a goddamn date." Idiot.

"Nobody knows me here. I won't get in your way. I promise." He looked at me and something shifted in my chest. I ignored it.

"Is that the best you've got? Is that your best do-as-I-ask-because-I'm-cute look?"

"You think I'm cute?"

"I think you're a fucking distraction."

"Really?" He leaned back, tossed his book on the table and grinned at me. Smug bastard. I launched my booted foot at his crotch and let it land hard on the stool between his legs. His eyes widened and his expression faltered for a moment. We were silent for a while, watched Elton hustle the wannabes.

I felt hands on my foot and I looked up to see Cleveland inspecting my boot. "Problem?"

"Not really. Nice boots."

"Thanks. They're new." I smiled.

"Oh yeah?" He drawled. Another shift, an unwinding of sorts. The look in his eye. The tingle that was making its way up my leg. I was slipping into something.

"I had two days with nothing to do but wait. So I went shoe shopping among other necessary endeavors." I fingered the edge of his book, turned the spine my direction. *The Great Gatsby*.

"Good book," he said.

"I'll take your word for it."

And this was where things got strange or average depending. Cleveland and I talked. Mostly, I talked and he listened. He told me about the girl he was dating right before he went to jail. He said he made his peace with her moving on but it was obvious he was hurt by it. The conversation was good. It was normal. But I wasn't here for this. He was going to be a problem. I hoped I wouldn't have to hurt him.

I caught myself wondering what kissing his lips would be like. Broad shoulders and long muscled arms that ended in those massive hands.

"What? Why are you smiling?" he said.

"I was thinking I hope I don't have to hurt you."

"Oh yeah? But what else were you thinking?" We locked eyes for a long moment. I bailed first. He laughed, "Come on, tell me."

"Sorry, I don't talk dirty on the first date?"

"Oh, this is a date?"

"Close enough. A faux date then. We're in a bar. We don't know each other. We've talked books, movies, religion and politics. In my limited experience I'd say we look like we're on a date."

"So you haven't dated much?"

"Not really. I just got out of something."

"Somebody let you go?"

"Yeah. It happens."

"Sure. So what do you do on a real first date."

"You wish you knew."

"Of course." He gently lifted my foot, got down off his stool, then leaned in close to my ear. His breath ghosted across my ear, "Ten years is long time to dream about a woman like you." He pulled back to survey the effect. Such a bad line. He had me and he knew it. I was a sucker. "Can I get you more water? Or beer?" he asked.

I started to respond but Elton beat me. "Get me one man." I saw Cleveland's good mood edge away. It was in the blink. Like a reset button. Back to the business at hand. He did it though. On the way back, some newly-broke college kid backed into him. The kid apologized but Cleveland stared down the guy for a moment too long and it was obvious something was going to happen. I jumped up and put myself between them.

"Hey, let's go sit." I pulled a beer from his hand and wound my fingers through his, pulling him back to our table.

"Problem?" Elton asked.

"No." Cleveland and I said in unison.

"Come on Elton, play one game with me then we'll get out of here." Lonnie purred and off they went. Cleveland glared at them.

"And now you're becoming a fucking problem," I said to him.

He sat down and I returned my foot to its prior position between his legs. "When are you gonna do this?" he said.

"Don't know yet. Don't worry about it." I was sure I'd get a chance. An opening always showed itself.

"You don't know? How can you not know?" He leaned forward, clamping his hands down on my foot and leg.

"You know what? Fuck this and fuck you." I yanked my foot away, grabbed my purse and walked past him, determined to exit out the back door.

This was a mistake. I should have listened to Frank. But I just had to prove myself. To who though? Myself? Frank? Maybe, but really to Simon. To show him I could function as well if not better than when I was with him. But I was wrong. I'm off my game and I should have stayed in Vegas. I had to get out now before this went completely off the rails.

I made it to the out-of-order pool table when a hand closed around my bicep and Cleveland pulled me to him.

"You can't just leave." His voice was rough with the effort to keep it low.

I faced him. "We had an agreement. You broke it, I still tried to accommodate you and now you wanna question my methods? You explain to Eileen why I left or do it yourself then. I don't need the aggravation." I tried to yank my arm away but he had me firm. I backed up until my ass hit the table.

"I'm not trying to fuck this up I just—" He glanced back. We could see Lonnie and Elton, oblivious to us still. "I hate seeing them like that. Happy like that when Tom's dead. He didn't deserve what happened to him."

I knew I shouldn't. But this guy, he was moving something in me and I realized it was too late to back away now. "I thought you wanted a little payback for Eileen. For your friend."

"I do," he whispered.

I rested my hand on his chest and rubbed. His grip on my arm loosened but I didn't pull away. I glanced around him to see Lonnie headed our way. "Then trust me."

He nodded.

"Good. Come here." I kissed him. I knew Lonnie would be watching. Figured it would be enough to convince her we were fine. I wasn't prepared for the kiss though. Any control I had was gone. He pressed me to him and stole my breath. I felt myself being lifted, turned. I wrapped my arms around his neck and settled in to the kiss. My hands in his hair, his arm firm around my waist. I lost track of time. Then I heard Lonnie. I tried to take a step back to break our kiss but he pulled me back and wrapped his other arm around me and I couldn't help but lean harder into him. The kiss was long and slow and deeper than I had intended. Finally, he let me go, let an inch of space form between us. I was dizzy and he looked as shell-shocked as I felt.

"Sorry."

"Don't be. It's been awhile, huh?"

Sheepish grin, "Yeah."

"Y'all need a room?" Lonnie leaned against the edge of the pool table and took us in. I had no doubt we were convincing.

"Go away." Cleveland all but growled at her.

"Sorry," I said. She shrugged gave Cleveland a disappointed look and walked away. I held his face in my hands. "Last time. Let me do this my way. Trust me. And don't get in my way. Fuck me over on this, get me noticed by the police and I swear I will sever an artery in you."

He started to smile but then something in my eyes must have convinced him I was serious. I liked the guy, more than I should but I had no intention of doing time for the crime he wanted committed. He nodded.

"Good let's go make nice." I pulled away but he remained seated. I raised an eyebrow.

"I'm gonna need a minute," he said, making a small gesture towards his crotch.

"Don't be long."

Another minute and he's at my side. We slipped into our roles as new couple seamlessly. His arm around my waist, my fingers through his belt loop.

Finally, it was one a.m. and we were bleary-eyed and I knew I was too tired. Too much alcohol. Too much Cleveland. Lonnie was cuddled up to Elton and I wanted to do the same to Cleveland. Just wrap myself around his body and dig in.

Lonnie turned to us. "There's a place up the way. We're going. You can come if you want." She was hyper and I began to wonder if at some point when I was busy with Cleveland if she had taken something. Either that or Elton's fabulousness had revved her motor up to this high-speed version. She bounced and fidgeted at his side.

Cleveland and I made excuses and headed out first. Cleveland walked me to my rental. He backed me up against it, dipped his face lower to look me in the eye.

"You know, there's a good chance that Elton is gonna do what Eileen wants done," I said. My fingers crawled under his shirt, rubbed along the skin they found.

"You mean once Lonnie pays Elton?"

"Yeah."

He pulled my hands away from his waist. "I need to make sure. Eileen needs to be sure."

From across the parking lot I heard Lonnie laugh. They talked for a minute at Elton's vehicle then they separated.

"Okay. Get in." I let him drive.

We followed them. A mile down the road, Elton's car turned into the parking lot while Lonnie continued past then she parked. She didn't get out. We stopped a fair distance away.

"You're gonna do this now? What about him?"

I figured Lonnie didn't want anyone to know she did more than share a few drinks with Elton. Or maybe Elton wanted to distance himself from her. Who knew? I had a window and I was determined to slip through it.

"Guess Eileen is gonna get the stone's throw special. Drive past and park down the street. I'll meet you after." From behind the driver's seat I pulled a small black backpack. In it there was the butcher's knife and the smaller knife. I got out and ran. The street wasn't lit well enough to see more than a shadow if anyone was looking. I watched Cleveland drive away. The headlights illuminated Lonnie's car a half block down. I made my way to the parking lot and around the corner of the building. Elton made his way from the office. I waited. He moved his car to an end stall, got out and opened the door directly in front of his car.

I needed to be in the room before Lonnie. I quick-walked down the walkway and knocked softly on the door. My backpack had a side zipper for convenience on the go. I pulled the larger knife out exposing just the handle through the opening. Elton opened the door, a cell phone in his hand, and surprise on his face.

"You."

"Hey," I said, giggling a little. "Lonnie and I thought it might be fun if we all played together tonight. Do you mind?"

He looked me up and down again. "She didn't mention it."

"Surprise." I figured I have three minutes tops before Lonnie showed. Call it two.

"Come on." He turned and I followed him in. I shut the door behind me, twisted the lock. Before it shut, the knife was in my hand. When Elton turned around, I was there with the knife. In at the belly and a sharp pull upward. Then stepped away. Elton fell to his knees gripping his bleeding torso. He was wide-eyed and confused. Gently, I pushed him over. Blood flowed over his hands. From his waistband, a gun fell heavy to the floor.

"You were gonna kill her, weren't you?"

He gurgled. I sank the knife into his chest. We each only had a moment, one moment before he took his last breath and another before Lonnie opened the door. I picked up the gun, turned off the light and left the door cracked. A sliver of light from the parking lot cut through a corner of the room. Down next to Elton; used my left hand to mimic him shooting with his right.

Lonnie arrived, pushed the door open. "Elton?" She walked in. One step. Two. "Oh my God, Elton."

I fired and the sound was louder than I expected. The bullet found a home in her chest. Good enough from the gurgling sounds she was making. I shut the door. Lonnie had fallen to the right and slumped down the wall. Carefully, I closed my hand over her mouth and pinched her nose shut. She was gone in less than a minute. From her purse, I pulled a fat envelope. The money. I placed it on the dresser, bills exposed. The door opened behind me. I turned; Elton's gun was still in my hand. Cleveland was in the doorway, backlit by the parking-lot lights. I couldn't see his face. I was exposed. I didn't want to shoot him.

"Let's go," he said, "we need to go before someone comes."

He turned slightly and now I could see his face. He looked a little concerned but relieved too. I set the gun back down at Elton's side and we left. No one saw us. Maybe they were used to gunshots. Maybe everyone was still at the bar.

I drove us back to my hotel. In my room, I stripped off my clothes. The blood on me was minimal. I bagged my clothes for the garbage later.

I found Cleveland sitting on the edge of the bed. He called Eileen on the way here. I could hear her crying. He was gentle with her. Talking to her in soothing tones. Now he looked exhausted. The night's tension had left its mark on his face. Deep shadows under his eyes.

He looked guilty. Guilty maybe because he was alive and his friend, some kid he got to know in letters, was dead and no amount of killing was going to change that.

Maybe he was frightened of the possibilities. A life. To find his new path, maybe a family and kids. Those things weren't lost to him yet. He wasn't me. He wasn't hung up on some old love.

I took his face in my hands and kissed him. I let him hold me, let him tell me again about his friend. I didn't wake him when I left the next morning. No goodbyes.

19

It was 110 out, the air conditioning was off and every window open. The late summer heat blew in through the front door and back out through the kitchen window. I was sweating and cleaning the house. Doing all those little things that I rarely did: wiping down counters, mopping the floors, running the washer, when the landline phone rang. I stopped with the mop, wiped my forehead on my sleeve and looked at the blue plastic phone jangling its ass off on the kitchen wall.

No one ever called me here. Not that I didn't have friends who might call—okay I didn't have friends—but the few work people who had the number still called the cell. My heart did a little stuttered beat. Dread, fear and hope did its work on my system in the time it took me to walk across the kitchen and get to the phone. I picked up on the fifth ring.

He said, "Meet me," and I was weak-kneed. Simon was calling me and asking me, his pliant ex, to meet him. I've done this before, come when he called and the sex had been hard, rough and painful. And worth every minute it lasted. Then he married her anyway and had me dispose of a guy in the desert. So I should know better. Besides, his tone wasn't quite what I want to hear. I wanted his tone to translate into, "Come fuck me." It was more, "I need to talk." But I'd take it, so I said okay.

After he found me two years ago, right after I'd killed a man and ostensibly had killed any possibility for a happy ending, he made a habit of taking me out drinking at least once a week. He wanted to see me let go, he'd said. I'd let go, all right. Drinking until I was numb, partying with whoever got too close to my gravitational pull. I'd swept up more than one man at those bar nights. Simon never let it go too far though. Always bundled me up and took me to his home, our home and tucked me carefully into bed. The next morning he'd bend me six ways to Sunday, grunting out his ownership of me, making me swear I was his and only his. I always swore my allegiance to him and I always went drinking again when he asked. Around the time I stopped getting smashed blind was about the time he introduced me to Frank. I guess he wanted to break me. Maybe he wanted me to be fully under his thumb and begging for him.

I changed my clothes then got in my truck and drove as fast I could to the bar. The Mighty-Mighty was dead and one or two of the regulars who sat at the bar looked dead too. They didn't even register my appearance as I whipped past them and the bartender on my way into the bathroom. I checked my face, washed my hands. The smell of bleach still lingered on my skin.

I inspected my shirt and stood in the way back so I could see my ass in the mirror. My jeans were just a little tight and showed it off well. I figured Simon wouldn't be inspecting me very closely just yet. If at all.

Happy with my looks I walked calmly out and surveyed the drunks. Simon was at the bar, grinning at me. He saw me come in. Damn.

I waved, inhaled and headed over to him.

"Hello, beautiful," he said. He didn't get up nor turn to look at me. He just kept smiling at our reflected faces.

"Hey."

He patted the stool next to him and signaled to the bartender. "Another beer."

I didn't sit. "There's a booth open in the back." Way in the back, in the deep shadows where no one could see us.

"Sorry I don't have that kind of time tonight. Have a seat."

"Oh," I said. Undeterred, I purposely bumped my shoulder into his as I sat down. He rocked away from me then back again. The bartender brought the beer then shuffled down to the other end of the bar.

"You look good. Comfortable," he said.

"You too," I said and tried to find the gray in his hair. But there wasn't any. He did look good.

"So about why I called you." He pushed his empty bottle away. I waited. "It's about the house."

We'd been broken up over a year. He was married now, living miles away from me in a swank new house. I figured the tiny railroad cottage was mine to live in.

"You want me out?"

"No," he said sharply, his head snapping up and turning my direction. "It's just that Marjorie thinks we should rent it out." He trailed off.

I couldn't stand him hiding behind her. Marjorie said this, Marjorie thinks that.

"But I guess she wouldn't want you to rent it to me? Right?"

"Laura," he said.

"No, it's fine." I took a swig of my beer and pushed off my stool.

"Let me finish. Sit down."

"Nah," I said, feeling the cold rush of the beer freeze me solid. I could be ice with him. I could do this. I could move on. "I'll be out by the end of the week."

If he watched me leave I didn't know it. I never turned around.

***

On my way home, I hit every grocery store between the bar and the house, asking for boxes. It wasn't a load night in most of them but I got what I needed. The next morning, I

106

busied myself and contemplated my options as I packed up books, the few dishes I owned and began the washer for the last two loads. The doorbell rang then a short rapid knock. Through the curtain I saw Simon's silhouette.

I could not answer. Let him stay on the outside; let him see what it was like. But before I could decide I heard his key in the lock, the doorknob turned and he was in front of me. But he looked like hell.

He was in the same clothes from last night. They were rumpled, definitely slept in. He hadn't shaved and, as he closed distance between us, I caught a whiff of alcohol.

"What happened to you?" I asked. I backed away trying to put a little distance between us. Not that I had an escape route.

"Why do you have to be so fucking difficult?" He shoved me hard against the wall, his hands on my biceps pinned me in place. A moth on display for the flame.

"How am I the problem here?"

He held me there a moment longer. Then he released me. "The house is yours."

"What?"

He pulled a folded paper from his pocket. "Just sign. And the house is yours."

"Why?"

He looked around. Boxes everywhere, the evidence of my morning's work was everywhere. "Because you belong here."

He dropped the paper on top of a box and let himself out.

20

I woke to rain beating at the windows and someone banging on my front door. I stumbled half awake down the hall and yelled "Who is it?" The banging stopped. Muffled but a distinct, "Cleveland." I opened the door.

Cleveland Tully stood before me. I hadn't seen this man for close to a year. He was soaked. His T-shirt clung to his body. His hair, longer than before, lay plastered to his head.

"Hey Laura," he said easily, smiling at me, while the rain slanted in under the eaves of my house and continued to drench him.

"What are you doing here? How did you find me?" I shivered in my doorway.

"Whoa, wait. Can I come in? It's kinda wet out here." He took a step towards me.

"Answer the question first." Somewhere in the house, my cell phone rang. In the kitchen, next to my purse, next to the knives.

"Which one?"

I pushed the door closed. He put out a hand out.

"Okay. I've been looking for you for a while now. Ever since you disappeared on me. For months nothing then boom, there you are. The new owner of this house."

That fit. I've only had the house for a few months. He continued, "I just thought I'd drop by. Say Hi. Ask you to dinner maybe. Or for coffee. Or for a beer and a game of pool." He lifted his eyebrows at the reference to our shared history. "You haven't forgotten our time together, have you?"

As if forgetting was possible. An assignment in Portland. A murderous wife and this troublemaker. Kissing in a bar, sex in a nice hotel bed. Yeah, I remembered Cleveland Tully. I smiled at him.

"Now can I come in?"

I stepped back, only intending to let him go past me. I figured we'd talk. I'd give him a towel. Maybe make some coffee. Instead, I'd barely shut the door when he pressed me to the wall. He leaned down and water dripped on my face. His lips were cold. His hands were colder as they reached under my shirt and fingers found skin. I could have protested. There was a small part of me that was saying What the fuck? But he wasn't someone I was afraid of. If he was anything he was pleasant memory and a few x-rated dreams. He picked me up and we moved down the hallway with me directing in between kisses, my legs wrapped his waist. He tossed me on the bed. He pulled off wet clothes. In his underwear he clambered over me and under my blankets pulling me in with him.

The cordless phone next to me began to bleat. He kissed me harder, my legs wrapped around him. He pulled my shirt over my head and began to kiss and nip down my neck. The phone kept ringing.

"Shit," I said.

"Ignore it," he mumbled into my neck.

"It's important."

He stopped at my collarbone. "How would you know it's important if you don't know who it is?"

I panted a little. His hair, drier now, was beginning to curl again.

"Only three people have the house number and only a few more have my cell phone number. It rang earlier and now this one is, so it's important." I reached for the phone. "Hello?"

"You are home. Why didn't you answer the cell?"

Simon. I squeezed my eyes shut and struggled to control myself while Cleveland continued to work his way across my torso. Hot breath played across a nipple and I nearly squealed.

"What do you need?" I said.

"For you to come in."

I bit off a moan and struggled in vain to pull Cleveland's face up and away. "Please," I whispered. He disappeared under the blanket.

"Are you okay?" Simon asked.

"Yes. When do you want me there?"

"Couple of hours."

"A couple of hours?" I glanced at the clock. 5:30 a.m. The blanket was flung off to reveal Cleveland now at my hip shaking his head vehemently.

"I can't, Simon. Tonight?"

There was a long pause. "You're not alone," Simon said.

Cleveland latched on to the waistband of my underwear with his teeth and began to work them down. I smiled. "No."

"Tomorrow morning. Be here at six. Have fun." He hung up. I tossed the phone in the general direction of the nightstand.

"That your boss?" He used his hands to pull my underwear off.

"Yeah, that was Simon."

"The old boyfriend." He ran his fingers down my thighs.

"Yes"

"Must be hard working for him. Is he always so hands on with you?"

I watched as he pulled off his underwear. "We mostly keep our distance. Nothing's easy."

"Does he still have feelings for you?" He stretched out across me, now fully naked. He pushed strands of hair from my face.

"I don't know. Why are we talking?" I squirmed but he held me in place under him. Not that leaving was my goal. I was twitching with need. It had been months since anyone was this close to me. Now that I thought about it, Cleveland was the last man in my bed. I wondered briefly what that meant when he sideswiped me with his next question.

"Do you still have feelings for him?"

I went rigid. I didn't have the words to explain Simon. The reasons why I stayed around him. I settled for, "It's complicated."

"Yeah, I get that."

Then he kissed me again and any urgency I had for a quick fuck dissolved away into seemingly endless kisses. Then he was in me, long slow strokes that brought me to edge repeatedly then finally over it.

After, I admitted, "I guess I missed you."

He laughed, his arms around me, body spooned next to mine and his face buried in my hair.

21

The clock read 5:13 a.m. when I rolled out of bed Saturday morning. Cleveland snored face down on the two-thirds of the bed he took up. He looked good twisted up in my bed sheets. The fading farmer's tan on his arms and the long expanse of pale skin called to me, urged me to come back to bed. To make him my breakfast. But I was late. So I had coffee instead on my way to see Simon.

I arrived ten minutes late but ready to deal with whatever he wanted. Ready to deal because whatever he wanted, he was gonna have to get somebody else to do it. Or at least wait until Monday. I wanted, needed, a few days off with Cleveland. The intensity of the attraction, the slow burn that I was walking around with, was strange to me. Strange because Simon was the only other person to make me feel this strongly. Maybe Simon was finally leaking out of my system.

The door to Pritchard Investigations' office suite was open. I walked into Simon's office, then came to a shuffling stop. Frank sat behind Simon's desk and he looked decidedly unhappy.

"Have a seat."

"Tell me what I did first." I hung on to the door handle. Strained to hear if other people were in the suite. Coming up behind me.

"Nothing Laura. You've done nothing wrong. Sit."

"Where's Simon?" Panic shot through me. Something had happened to Simon. I shut the door behind me and sat across from Frank in the suede armchairs.

"Simon is fine."

I exhaled one long breath. Relief rolled through me and I set my coffee down. I was jittery now and definitely awake.

"Tell me about your house guest."

"What?"

"The guy in your bed right now."

This wasn't happening. "Simon has you digging around my bedroom now? I thought you wouldn't stoop to that. Thought you had better things to do." Never once in the nearly four years I have known him has Frank ever gone out on a legit case. He never did surveillance on anybody unless they were going to end up dead by the end of it. I got up, shaking my head, disappointed.

Frank's hands, out of sight since I walked in, now rose slowly into view. The right hand hefted a gun, setting it down gently. The left pointed its fingers at me and directed me back to my chair. The gun wasn't pointed at me exactly, just in my general direction. The muzzle tapped the cherry wood desktop.

"What the hell, Frank." I took a seat again.

"How do you know him?"

"That Portland job."

Frank thought hard. His forty-year-old gears turned slowly on some things. Other things, like his trigger finger were just as quick as they ever were. His face lit up. "The guy who attacked you in the parking garage? You're fucking that guy? Don't you think that might be a mistake?"

It's hard to hold that against a guy when we attacked each other in a hotel room a day later. "Why the gun?" I asked.

He ignored my question. "Laura, this boyfriend of yours, you've been seeing him for a while?"

I explained the last time I saw him and his unexpected arrival yesterday.

"What's he been doing?"

"Fucking half the state of Oregon for all I know. Why? What is going on?"

Frank got up. The gun was down at his side when he walked over to me. I sat rigid, waiting for...whatever. He stood before me, leaned down and took my chin in his left hand. I barely held back the flinch. An eternity passed. Then he nodded as if he had seen something in my face, some proof of something, and the gun disappeared. He sat back on the edge of the desk. I slumped back in my chair.

"Your new boyfriend was sent to kill Simon." He said it just like that. It was an everyday thing, someone trying to kill Simon. My Simon.

My Cleveland. My Simon. My head began to hurt.

"Not possible," I said.

"No, it's true. And he's worse than you were when you first started. A rental car in his name outside of Simon's house. He approached Marjorie at a casino. Just said hello, nothing menacing. She remembered him because of that baby face of his." I winced at the mention of Simon's wife. A statuesque blonde who had moved in on Simon and replaced me in the space of a weekend. Eight months later they were married.

"He's using you to get close to Simon. Has he asked about him?"

Last night's conversation came back to me. Must be hard working for him. Why do you stay? Does he still care for you? Jesus, was he trying to gauge my reaction? Was he calculating the odds of me coming after him? Or maybe helping him?

"Not really. Just wondered how I could work for my ex."

"Now there's a question never to be answered." He met my look with one of his own. He won. "Keep an eye on him. Let me know if he leaves your side, okay?"

My head pounded on. "I need to talk to Simon. Where is he? He called me because of a job, right?"

"We turned the job down. Simon isn't here. Go home. Keep the boyfriend in bed. Pretend you don't know anything."

"Who wants Simon dead?"

A shrug.

"Who did he piss off?"

"It doesn't matter Laura. It's being dealt with."

"Does Simon know who ordered it? He's gonna get them to call it off?" I rubbed my forehead. "This isn't happening."

"Do what you're told, Cupcake. This is happening but we are gonna deal with it and get through it. Go. Home."

22

I was nearly home when I decided I couldn't go in. I drove past my driveway, took a left at the end of my street and parked. Deep breaths. Slow, deep breaths. It couldn't be true. But Frank wouldn't lie. I couldn't see how a lie would benefit him.

Okay, see the angles. Simon called. He wanted me for something. Got me panting in his ear while another man licked my stomach.

Jealousy?

Anger?

A lie?

An excuse to get rid of Cleveland? I couldn't be mad if he was trying to hurt Simon. A lie. An extravagant one, though. To take off, turn down work? Fuck it. This was about Simon. Proving that he's the biggest dick in the room. This almost fit. I could almost convince myself.

I went home and found Cleveland only slightly different from when I left him earlier. He was face up now. A muscular arm draped over his face fended off the brightening morning. The sheet rode low on his hips and I paralleled the light trail of hair on his belly with kisses, down to where it disappeared and beyond.

***

We spent the day together sightseeing—Fremont Street, Container Park. We ate at a new restaurant and strolled through gambling floors with the rolling tones of digital hands being dealt as our music. It wasn't magical. This was Vegas. It was neon and bright and made me want to crawl out of my skin. Too many people and too many lights. That night I didn't sleep.

So what kept me up? The insistent whine of doubt. Doubt put there by the Simon-in-hiding routine and reinforced by Frank's little bombshell. Doubt wasn't a seed that grew but a swarm of mosquitos, buzzing, whispering and sucking my confidence in Cleveland away little by little.

By four a.m. I was done. I was sure I knew where Simon was. It's the only place I knew to look and if he wasn't there then I didn't know where to look. Maybe I'd go to his wife. Wouldn't that be great, "Hello, Marjorie. My, your tan looks swell. Have you seen your husband in the last two days? He thinks my boyfriend wants to kill him. Did he mention it?"

I slipped from under Cleveland's warm body. Maybe it was the sudden change in temperature or the distinct difference between my body and the mattress but he woke.

"Hey, everything okay?" He had deep lines on one side of his face, creases from the sheets. I sat next to him. Kissed him. Urged him to go back to sleep.

"Simon needs me for something." His eyebrow rose. "Not to worry, Simon gets those things taken care of by his proper wife now."

"But you get up at," he rolled over to see the clock, "four in the goddamn morning?"

I shrugged. "He calls, I answer. It's just the way it is."

"The way you let it be." He sat up now. "I don't understand."

"You don't have to. It's not a requirement." I rose, found jeans, sweatshirt and socks and pulled them on. I went head first into my closet searching for my hiking boots. I heard the bed creak and then he pulled me from behind and turned me over to look at me.

"I'm not here to fight with you," he said, sitting down on the floor with me.

"Good."

"Laura, you just bow down to him. What does he have over you?"

I went back into the closet and finally found the shoes I had been looking for. "Nothing. He's my boss. And I'm loyal."

"To a fuckin' fault."

I scooted back away from him. "Go back to sleep. You'll be less grumpy later. I have to go."

"What if I say you can't go?"

"I'd say don't be here when I get back." And I walked out, my shoes in hand.

On a whim, I drove down the street then circled back to the house. The bedroom light was on now, a dim, yellow square of light on the side of the house. I drove on.

It was silly but I had to be sure. I went to the office. Building security eyed me and my untied hiking boots, but said nothing. Up in our offices, it was quiet. Simon's chair sat empty. I sat down and had to push away the visceral memories of our past. It'd been over a year since he touched me but damn if it didn't rise up at me like it was yesterday. His scent, the expanse of his bare chest. Fuck.

I shook my head and turned on his desk lamp. The desk, clean of clutter, gleamed in the light. All the drawers were locked. It wouldn't have taken much to open them but why bother. Simon wasn't here. Hadn't been here. I called Simon's business cell phone. His voicemail was full. Guess I wasn't the only one who wanted to talk to him.

I heard the ding of the elevator. I stopped moving and listened to footsteps. Whoever it was didn't care if I knew they were coming or didn't know I was here. I turned off the light. On the other side of Simon's frosted glass door a large figured loomed, the edges indistinct then became solid. The door swung open. The security guard from downstairs smiled at me. A mistake, because no one's snaggle-toothed smile could ever make me feel at ease.

"Just wanted to make sure you were still here," he said, positioning himself in the opening. I stood and came around the desk.

"Why is that?"

"You need to stay for just a few minutes more, Ma'am."

"Is that right?" I considered the door and the guard. Positioned half in like he was, I could kick the door. But I'd probably put my foot through it, hurting myself more than him. I stepped closer to him. "I don't really feel like staying any longer," I said. From my purse I pulled my baton. I pushed the release button and let it telescope to its full length. The guard's eyes widened. I really thought he might back down. But no.

"I'm supposed to keep you here and you're not leaving." He pulled a taser off his belt and his own police issue baton. "Sit down."

When I didn't he came fully into the room, shutting the door behind him. I stepped toward him. He raised the taser. I feinted left, dropped down and flung my baton as hard as I could. The taser probes missed me. Too bad for him that I didn't miss too. The baton caught him in the face. It was enough to leave him unfocused for the necessary seconds I needed to get up and throw my body into his, sending us both into Simon's door. As the glass broke he screamed. How nice was he to break my fall with his body? I punched him in the face as a thank you, quite satisfied with the sound of his head hitting the floor repeatedly. I straddled his body and my foot hit his baton. I lifted it and gave him a smile of my own.

"Jesus lady. I'm sorry," he said through a bloodied mouth. He put his hands up in defense, coverering his face.

"You oughta be," I said. I raised the baton intending to give him a few more reasons to be sorry but the elevator's ding made me stop. I looked down the hallway and saw Marjorie Pritchard's blonde, tanned, high-heeled self walking towards me.

"Mrs. Pritchard, I was trying to get her to stay," said the unfortunate guard.

"Oh, you've gotta be kidding me," I said. I dropped the baton and moved off the guard. I picked my way through the glass and returned to Simon's chair and turned on his lamp.

The guard stood, brushed himself off. "She came at me."

"It's all right, Louis. I'll deal with her."

Deal with me? This should be entertaining. She stepped carefully through the broken door's frame. She smiled and sat down across from me. The reason for Simon's attraction was obvious. This glowing blonde, sleek muscled body, buffed into perfection.

"That's my husband's chair you're sitting in." She crossed her pale legs and her skirt rose up another inch.

"Where is your husband?"

"You don't know?"

"I wouldn't ask if I did, Marjorie."

"Mrs. Pritchard." She waved her hand at me. The diamond and platinum ring sparkled in the lamplight.

"Yes, yes. Mrs. Pritchard. But do you know where your husband is?"

"Why are you doing this?"

"What?"

"Pining after a man you'll never have."

"I had him once."

"And you'll have him again? No, you won't." She leaned forward, "Besides that new boy of yours is cute."

I nodded hating that she had taken control of the conversation. I exhaled a long breath. "So you're paying security to watch me now?"

"Louis is convenient."

"But useless."

"Simon tells me nothing about this place. I'm sure you'll be happy to know that he won't talk about you."

"He doesn't talk about you either." I got all my information from his secretary.

"Why don't you leave?" she asked.

I belong here, I started to say. But maybe that wasn't true. It didn't matter though. I needed to find Simon and straighten things out.

"Look, I need to talk to Simon so do you know where he is or not?"

"Of course, I do. He's at the cabin. I'm sure that misguided boyfriend of yours will drive you up there to talk to him as soon as you leave."

I stood up. "When did you talk to Cleveland?"

"Downstairs, in the parking garage. Where he's waiting for you. He asked where Simon was and I told him where but that if he was serious about you that he should convince you to leave Las Vegas. He's a smartass like you though. He said maybe Simon should let you go. Like he's the one holding on to you. Where are you going?"

I ran out of the office and down to the elevator. Two long minutes later I was in the parking garage and Cleveland was nowhere in sight. I figured he had a twenty-minute head start on me but I couldn't just go after him unarmed. Frank long ago gave me a gun. I never used it but I kept it loaded and close to my bed.

I went home and unlocked my front door and heard the footsteps behind me too late. The punch knocked me into the door, breaking the glass panels. Then the door opened. I looked up, tried to focus on the man. There was a small part of me that was happy it wasn't Cleveland.

"Hello," he said then pulled me up by the hair and the collar. He dragged me backward down the hallway and tossed me onto the couch. Another man sat in on one of my uncomfortable kitchen chairs. Longish black hair, wire brushes for eyebrows.

"Where is Cleveland?" he asked.

"Do you have a name?"

"Mignard."

"Laura. Why are you in my house?"

"Last time, where is Cleveland?"

"I thought he was here. I don't know where he is."

"Where is Simon Pritchard?"

"I don't know?"

"I should believe you?"

"I don't have a lot of reasons to lie."

"When did you see Cleveland last?"

"He was here."

"And Pritchard?"

"Not since Tuesday. I spoke to him Friday morning though."

"I should believe you?"

"Yes."

He smoothed an eyebrow down. "Okay. You give Cleveland a message. Tell him a week is too much time. We expected more." He got up then. He was nearly gone. But I was angry that they were in my house. No one had ever hurt me here.

"Maybe you should have hired a pro then."

He stopped in mid-stride and swung his head back at me. "What was that?"

"I said, maybe you should've gotten a pro."

He sat back down. "Like you?"

"I'm better than Cleveland."

"You are Simon's old girl. Right? Now he is with the blonde in Spanish Hills. In the big house overlooking the golf course, right? And you live here, in this box." One of his men laughed. "Yet you work for him still. I heard about you. You are his dog." He waited for my reaction. And the effort it took not to give him one was mighty.

He went on, "Like me. Like them," he gestured to his men. "We are loyal. But you are foolish." He waggled a finger at me. Disappointed in my bad wannabe-thug behavior.

God, this was old. They obviously were after Cleveland and now it wouldn't matter if he did the job or not. He was in this deep, whatever this was. "Are we done?"

"Maybe I should kill you."

Now who's the talkative one? "Why do you want Simon dead?"

"Not me. But your employer should keep his fucking to his wife and you." I wished. But he hadn't touched me since before the wedding. We had had our moments of weakness, when proximity had proven too much and he pressed me up against the tall windows of his office. Simon could've had me any day of the week. But he never did.

"All of this is because he slept with someone?"

"Yes, the wrong woman. A price must be paid. He didn't take my employer seriously."

Simon. Simon. Simon. The son of a bitch was going to get us all killed over a piece of ass. "Can we make this right still?"

"Probably not. But try. You never know. I don't want us to be enemies. Maybe we will work together someday."

"Sure," I said. Maybe we could trade business cards too. I wondered if there was a trade union for made guys, bodyguards and hired killers. Something with the motto, "Have gun, will kill," our logo could be a German Shepherd no, it'd have to be a pit bull or Rottweiler.

He stood to leave again and this time I kept my damn mouth shut.

Cleveland's clothes were still in my bedroom. His duffel bag half open, a T-shirt hung out. I went to my headboard, reached behind the padded corner and felt the butt of the gun. I pulled out my Glock 17 and let it lie on the white sheets of my bed. A present from Frank. Something for my too small hands. Between Frank and Simon I was proficient with handguns but never used one outside of a practice range. On my way out I grabbed a serrated knife from the kitchen. I was happier with a knife. I drove to Mount Charleston.

23

When we were together, Simon took me up to his cabin on Mount Charleston a couple of times. It was a cozy log cabin that was bigger than the house we lived in together. He'd taken me out to teach me to shoot. Handguns and rifles. He'd given me a rifle, showed me how to line up the sight and prepared me for the recoil after the shot. I was never ready for it. But eventually I got good enough to taunt him into a competition. Then he'd grab Betty, his father's gun. His prized possession. I never touched it. No one did.

***

I drove past the lodge and up the curved dirt road that led to the cabin. Simon told me he felt safe there because he could see anyone coming up at him. Escape routes were minimal but on foot you could travel quite a ways without any problems. Within ten minutes I could see the cabin. No cars were in sight but I didn't expect there to be. Likely Cleveland would drive farther up and come back down on foot. Simon would park around back.

I found Cleveland's car farther up the road. I parked near it and ran back down the road and came up behind the cabin. I heard voices. The back door was open, kicked in. I peeked around the corner and caught a glimpse of Cleveland standing with his back to me. In front of him sat Simon, looking calm. Even. Looking like he was being entertained. I slipped in quietly but Simon saw me. His voice rose.

"What is this really about? You're trying to prove yourself?"

I crouched down behind the counter.

"She'll come with me," Cleveland said.

"Laura? You're doing this for her?"

"I didn't know she was going to be here, connected to you. She complicated things. But this is more than coincidence." This was fate, I heard him say. He believed in that. He'd told me all about it when we first met. Fate, that cosmic rightness to the world that put some people in the right place at the right time. He wanted me to come with him. Could I do that? Leave all of this behind? For what though? A life on the run from some version of a bad guy? Leave Simon? Let Simon die? I looked around the corner of the cabinets. Simon was standing now. They were the same height. Simon could've taken him if not for the gun. Simon let me go. He left me for her.

"She won't leave me. Kill me and she'll kill you."

"She'll come with me. She'll be upset for a while but our connection is too strong for her to ignore."

Simon laughed.

"I won't break her heart like you did."

I looked down at the gun in my hands. I knew my limitations. They were no more than twenty feet away from me. I stepped into the living room. In our training sessions Frank always said aim for the body.

My first shot went wide to the left. My second found a home in his leg. Then the gun jammed. I pulled the trigger but nothing happened. Amazingly, he never got a shot off. Simon stood over him now as he lay on the floor panting, cursing, bleeding. The front door exploded open and Frank was there, shotgun in hand. He jerked the gun up towards the ceiling.

"Laura." He looked from me to Cleveland and back again. The three of us stood over Cleveland, looking down at him.

"I need to know who sent him," Simon said. Cleveland stared hard at me. He didn't know that I knew. That I had the answer Simon needed. I leaned down and put my face close to his.

"I would've gone with you." It didn't feel like a lie. I looked up at Frank, "He'll tell you. Eventually."

***

Cleveland was screaming my name. I sat on the couch, my knees hugged to my chest. I rocked back and forth while Simon paced and smoked behind me. With every pass, his fingers stroked my hair. Finally, he found something worthy to say. "What you did…you did good today." His hand was warm on my head. Almost comforting. He caused this, though.

I shrugged out of Simon's reach. Frank emerged from the bedroom, Cleveland's lingering voice wafted out with him. He'd been working on Cleveland for an hour. Simon made him shut the door after he broke his fingers.

"He says he doesn't know who wants you dead, only the man who paid him. Some guy, I don't know the name."

"I'll talk to him," Simon said.

Frank went to the kitchen, removed my gun from his waistband and put it on the counter. I watched him wash his hands of Cleveland's blood. I closed my eyes. I needed to stop this. From down the hall, I heard Simon talking to him. I unlocked my limbs and walked up behind Frank. He'd gotten himself a glass and was gulping water. Torture was hard work. I reached out to touch his shoulder and saw my hand tremble.

Frank said, "I'm sorry, Cupcake."

"You followed me. Did you really think I had something to do with this?"

"I didn't want to believe it. But I didn't have room to make a mistake. You didn't want to believe me. And if you weren't part of it, I figured you'd want to know the truth."

He knew it would eat at me, the not being sure. He knew I had to pursue this.

"But I am sorry." Frank didn't apologize. Not to me. Not to anyone. He'd never given the impression that he knew what it meant to be sorry. He turned and I stepped away. He pulled me back to him and wrapped his other arm around me. He didn't realize I was reaching for the gun. I went up on tiptoe and kissed his cheek. My fingers curled around the gun's grip. I slipped away from his embrace.

"It's okay," I said.

"Laura."

I went down the hallway and grabbed a pillow as I went. He didn't follow. I wondered what he thought I'd do. Kill Simon maybe? No, I had my chance for that.

The door was open. Their poses were reversed from earlier, Simon over Cleveland this time. But again the sitting man had seen me first. He made a sound, a low moan. He knew why I was there. I stepped between them and placed the pillow gently over his face, squeezed the trigger. Simon yanked me back. Frank came running. I didn't look at Simon. This was all his fault.

"Jesus," Simon said.

I handed the gun butt first to Frank. "The guy's name is Mignard. He works for someone who doesn't like the fact that Simon is fucking his girl." I heard a sharp intake of breath.

"You knew that all this time and you didn't say anything?" Simon said.

"He used me to get to Simon. He deserved this," I said to Frank.

"Yeah but I could have been on the phone already. Fixing this," Simon said.

I turned to look at him. "Fuck you." I wouldn't look at Cleveland's body but there was the horrible sound of dripping in the room. I tried to leave but Simon grabbed me.

"We'll take you home, just sit down." He walked me back to the couch and tried to make me sit down.

"Let her go," Frank said.

Simon did and I was in my truck and headed down the mountain without a backward glance.

***

No one came to the house Sunday night or Monday. I stayed in bed with Cleveland's things in sight. His luggage. His clothes. Sometime around midnight I got up. I stripped my bed of its sheets, balled them up with his clothes and loaded them up into my truck. I drove until I found what I wanted. An apartment complex just rundown enough not to notice me entering. I went to the back to find the dumpsters, overfilled with furniture and smelling awful. There was room in one and I stuffed Cleveland's belongings into it.

I returned home and showered, let the water wash over me. I stayed under until I was clean enough. As clean as I was ever going to get. I stayed until long after the water had gone cold. Then I dressed and drove to the office.

It was nearly six a.m. when I arrived. I wasn't surprised to see the lights on. I walked into Simon's office.

"Laura, what are you doing here?" Simon stood. Frank didn't seem surprised to see me.

"You had a job for me. It's not too late to accept it, is it?" I held out my hand. I just wanted the information so I could go.

"You don't have to, Laura," Simon said.

"Here, don't fuck it up okay." Frank shoved paper into my hand.

I smiled. "I won't." And I was off to Chicago.

24

Richard Miller was an embezzler, a skimmer, who had taken a little too much off the top. He was in Chicago for a convention. I was here for him.

I caught a cab to the bar that Miller had taken a liking to. Last call would be soon. I entered the bar, slid onto a barstool one away from Miller and ordered a whiskey. Miller leaned my way, one ass cheek off his stool. He stared hard into his drink. I wondered what was swirling around with his ice cubes. Sensing my eyes on him, he looked up. Our gazes locked in the mirror and I smiled slightly at him. Just a hello smile, not an 'I'm easy' smile. That would come later. Miller's interest returned to his drink.

The bartender showed up with my drink and Miller downed his own.

"Another," he mumbled. He gave his glass a shove and it slid perilously close to the edge before the barman caught it.

"I think you've had enough. Why don't you head home?" The barman's voice was pleasant but his face bore no trace of it. He was ready for a fight. Miller tried not to disappoint. But he was all bark.

"Hey, come on now," he said, "I've got money and I want a drink." Miller dug into the pockets of his pants then his coat. Finally, he produced his wallet and slapped cash on the bar.

The barman shook his head, said, "Last call," to the other patrons in the bar. To Miller he said, "Sorry, man."

"Ah, fuck you," Miller said sounding more like a petulant boy than a forty-year-old man. He tried to stuff his wallet back into his coat pocket and nearly tumbled off his stool with the force of his effort.

"Sir." I leaned over in his direction, my cleavage tilted dangerously. Miller got a good look before meeting my eyes. "How about you have my drink and then we'll call a cab. Okay?" I glanced at the bartender. He nodded and picked up the phone.

"You sure?" Miller asked. My drink was in his hand before he even finished asking the question.

"Sure. It wasn't what I was really after."

Miller raised the glass to me then swallowed my two fingers worth of whiskey in a single gulp.

"I'm Richard," he said.

Well, hello Dick. "Jane," I said and extended my hand to him. The bartender announced our cab was on its way, and we out into the cool night air.

On the bench in front of the bar, we sat shoulder to shoulder. I shivered and Miller took notice. Goosebumps dotted my exposed flesh and he looked like he might be interested in connecting the dots. To my cleavage, Miller asked, "What are you doing out this time of night?"

"I'm just out," I lied. "I'm single, again," I said, with a pout as the cherry on top.

"Divorced?" he asked my chest.

I nodded.

"Me too," he said.

I grinned at his lie and leaned into him, giving him the full impression of my breasts against his arm, while I stole his wallet. "You wouldn't want to come with me to my hotel, would you?" Time for the easy smile. Between the liquor and my cleavage, I was sure Miller wouldn't say no.

"Oh," he frowned and with effort looked me in the face. "I gotta work tomorrow. Been out too late as it is."

Shit.

"Too bad," I said. I leaned away and closed my coat. Across the street, the lights in a restaurant went off and two people exited into the alley, walked toward the street then turned left. We watched them disappear into the night. I looked back at the alley. A dumpster hulked in the dark. I turned to Miller and brushed my lips over his. "Come with me." His eyes went wide. Then he listened to the alcohol in his blood, took my hand and led me across the street to the alley.

Next to the foul-smelling dumpster, he shoved me up against the wall. He worked his wide, flat tongue into my mouth and his hands found their way inside my coat. I allowed his hands to grip my breasts. All that tease, I figured I owed him but kissing was not his forte. When his hands went too far, I pushed him back and we traded positions. My hand drifted to his buckle but he was impatient and pushed my hand away. He opened his pants and I reached up for him and took him in hand. Another moan like that would have someone thinking there was a dying animal back here. His head fell back against the wall and his eyes closed.

"Hush," I said a little harsher than I intended. Not that he noticed. He was too busy babbling. "Can't believe this. They're never going to believe this." I slid my hand up my thigh and pulled my knife from its sheath. I aimed for his femoral artery high on his thigh. Stabbed him twice and backed away quickly. He gasped and slid down the wall. Blood pumped from his leg. I walked away from him listening for people, traffic. The alley was quiet. Adrenaline was singing in my veins. My hands shook as I wiped them on my handkerchief. I slipped it, and the knife, into my pocket. I headed down the street, knowing Frank wouldn't be far. I'd made it a block when he pulled up beside me.

"Need a ride, little girl?"

"Shut up." I slid into the seat next to him.

"You did him in the alley? That couldn't have smelled good."

"Trust me, kissing him was really the unpleasant part."

"Your phone has been vibrating for so long I think your battery died."

He tossed my phone into my lap. I opened it and saw there was only one battery bar left. Twenty-six missed calls flashed at me. All were from the same number.

"Simon?"

"Yeah." I couldn't help but smile a little. If it was life or death, Simon would have called Frank. No, these twenty-six phone calls were all about me. He hated being ignored and I hadn't talked to him in three days. I turned the phone off and settled in for the drive to O'Hare. Six hours later we were home.

25

All those phone calls and now Simon had me waiting an hour. I paced his office nearly vibrating with frustration. When there was a job to do, I could wait all day. But now that we weren't together anymore, waiting for him was intolerable.

I stood in front of his floor-to-ceiling windows and looked out on the glittering spread of Las Vegas dressed in all its night finery, lit up like an airport runway, with the strobing lights directing the tourists to their casinos of choice. As my watch ticked over to six o'clock, Simon strode in with a cell phone pressed to his ear. He nodded at me and I sat down in the available chair across the desk from him.

At fifty years old, Simon Pritchard still had a lean, hard body, and a full head of hair, brown and graying slightly at the temples. I was sure he still did sit ups before bed, though likely not as many as when he was with me. Maybe that meant he'd mellowed some and accepted his age. Of course having a proper wife might have something to do with that. No more twenty-five-year-olds for him. Not that I was twenty-five anymore. I'd spent my last birthday, my thirty-fourth, doing a job for him. Now I just wanted to be paid so I could crawl into a tequila bottle and celebrate properly.

He ended his phone call and draped his coat over the chair beside me. Leaning back against his desk, he unbuttoned his suit jacket and folded his arms across his chest. I gave his body a long look before I looked up at his face. He smiled down at me.

"How are you?" he asked.

"I'm good," I said. There was the sudden hum of the air-conditioner kicking on and Simon's hair moved slightly in the new breeze. The scent of his woodsy cologne and a faint whiff of vanilla came in my direction. I pulled my eyes away from his face and began studying a crease in my skirt. Simon put me on edge and he knew it. Just being this close to him, close enough to smell him, would leave me shaking like a junkie overdue a fix. He'd taught me a lot during our five years together. Love, sex and misery. All of it I learned at the foot of his bed and, in the wake of his dismissal of me, I learned why some wives and husbands resorted to murder instead of just leaving. Sometimes love was too painful, and wishing someone a crappy life wasn't enough to pacify a broken heart.

"Any problems last night?" he asked.

"Miller was easy," I said without looking up. I remembered the sticky heat of his blood on my hands, the surprised look in Miller's eyes and how the life faded out of them as he slid down the wall.

"Laura." I looked up in time to see him reaching for me. I flinched. "I wouldn't hurt you. You know that." He cooed. I glared at him. "You know how I mean."

Right, because having sex with me the night before you got married wasn't going to hurt me.

"Sure. Just pay me so I can leave, please."

He went to his desk, unlocked a drawer and produced an envelope.

"So do you have plans for this evening?" He tapped his fingers on the envelope, still smiling his knowing smile. This was me after all, his lovesick ex. Too busy pining for him to have even bothered to find someone new, someone permanent, in the three years since our affair ended. It had taken me all the years and several temporary men to take the edge off my desire for him and while there wasn't someone waiting for me tonight, that didn't mean Simon needed to know it.

"Yesterday was my birthday. I have birthday sex I'm late for." I put out my hand to receive the envelope, smiling broadly at the flash of anger that crossed his face. He reached across his desk and dropped the envelope into my open hand. I drew it into my lap and glanced in. A bundle of bills and the printout of the money transfer sat snuggly inside.

Working for Pritchard Investigations was easy. Officially, I was on Simon's books as a consultant. I did a few assignments a year and the trail from the client to Simon and thus to me was so winding and varied that we were nearly untouchable. He paid me a percentage in cash and the rest was wired to an account. One day I would be done with this kind of work and I wanted to be smart about my retirement.

"As always, thank you." I stood to leave, dropping the envelope into my purse.

"Wait," he said. Opening another drawer, he retrieved a box, small and Tiffany-blue. He walked around to face me and handed me the box.

"Happy birthday. Sorry you had to work."

My mouth went dry. "Simon, I can't accept this."

"You haven't opened it yet. You can't refuse a present without knowing what it is."

I knew this was dubious logic but I opened the box anyway. Diamond earrings sparkled in the fluorescent lights of his office.

"It's not every day you turn thirty-four. You should have a nicer memory than last night to commemorate it." He stood closer now. "Put them on."

He held the box while I removed the tiny gold hoops that I usually wore and put in the diamonds. He pushed my hair back behind my ears and rested his hands on my neck. His thumbs described small circles on the skin. The pose was too intimate, too familiar and I knew I should step away but his gaze held mine and I wanted him to kiss me and destroy all the progress I'd made. I bit my lip and waited for his approval.

"You look good."

I nearly shivered with delight. I was such a fucking dog for him. Throw the ball, throw the ball, scratch right here and watch my leg twitch. Fuck me.

"They're beautiful. Thank you," I said.

"Come have a drink with me? I'd like to talk to you about another assignment." His hands were gone and I was momentarily thrown off balance. He grabbed his coat and gestured for me to do the same.

"Simon, I told you I have somewhere I need to be." I tried to put an edge into my voice.

He pulled another envelope from his desk. "This is what you were paid for the Miller guy. Upfront with another payment equal to it upon completion." He dropped the second envelope on the desk.

"For what? For who?" I flexed my fingers but left the envelope there. Simon tilted his head. I knew this tell. It meant he wasn't just uncomfortable but that the next words out of his mouth would most likely be a lie. I waited.

"It's a favor. What difference does it make?"

"Get somebody else." I scoffed. "I have plans." I put my coat on, intent on leaving.

"It's a favor for me. It's personal."

I looked at him. His shoulders slumped slightly. His usual air of machismo drifted off to parts unknown. Possibly, he was telling the truth now.

"It's for you?"

He nodded. By his posture I thought I knew what he wanted but I needed him to say it. I needed to hear from his own lips what he wanted.

"I miss you. I can't anymore—with her."

Her. His wife. I wanted to laugh in his face. I wanted to back out of the room. This was huge and the simple truth was I still wanted him. But I couldn't be stupid about this.

"Don't play me, Simon."

"I'm not. Look, I don't want her done messy. I just need her gone. You could do that." He stepped toward me hands apart, imploring me to listen and it was the proof of my affection for him that I didn't just leave. He met his wife at a dinner party held at the mayor's home. They were introduced and Simon—smelling money and opportunity—went to work wooing Miss Marjorie Adams. They were married within six months. Together they rubbed elbows with the affluent and wealthy that lived in and visited Las Vegas and through it Simon achieved another level of respectability for Pritchard Investigations. Her sudden demise would have the notable and powerful in town sniffing around Pritchard and in time, sniffing around me.

"Does Marjorie know about all of what you do here?"

"Some of it."

"Huh." I gazed at him and he moved closer. I shook my head. "Get someone else. It wouldn't be smart for me. Besides, I can't do your dirty work."

Simon moved as if he was going to step toward me again but instead he dropped into his chair.

"Fine," he said, defeat in his voice. He rubbed his hands over his face and through his hair. He looked old now, rumpled like that. I felt sorry for him but I left anyway.

26

Frank was sitting on my front porch when I got home. A package wrapped in brown paper sat on his lap.

"Where you been?" he asked.

"Simon gave me a birthday present." I unlocked my front door and kicked off my shoes as I headed to the kitchen. He shut the door. I pulled two tumblers from the cabinet. Frank was behind me when I turned around. He moved in close and sniffed.

"You don't smell like sex or soap."

"Shut up. Is that for me?"

He presented his package. Birthday wrapping paper, discount liquor store style. My present was a bottle of tequila.

He grinned at me. "So what did he give you for your birthday then?"

"Earrings." I poured too much into each glass, handed one to him and tossed back my own. Grimaced. Frank grabbed me by the neck, brushing back my hair and thumbing the earring.

"Nice."

I pulled away. "Yeah, they're okay."

"They cost some money. Are you sure he didn't give you anything else for your birthday?" His eyebrows rose suggestively.

"A proposition."

"I bet." He laughed and downed his drink.

Frank had taught me a lot over the years. How to inflict pain but more importantly, who to hurt. Not everyone deserved to suffer, he'd told me, only certain people. You'll know when you meet them. Now that I was less a student and more his equal, I was uncertain of him and the lines between us. But I knew I could trust him.

"He asked me to kill her."

Frank lowered his glass slowly. "What did you tell him?"

"What could I say? I told him no." I poured more tequila.

"Did he say why?"

"No and I didn't ask."

I made myself comfortable on my couch and Frank stood in the opening between the living room and kitchen. He was waiting for the details. This already felt like a betrayal somehow. Simon trusted me—to be his fool maybe. I knew what Frank would say. I told him anyway. When I was done, he swallowed his drink and poured us each another.

"Happy birthday, Cupcake." He crossed the to stand in front of me. He leaned down, his hand on my knee, fingertips just under the hem of my skirt. He had the oddest blue eyes I'd ever seen. They're a steely blue, like ball bearings. Those eyes worked to his advantage, not many people could look at him for any length of time.

"That's it? Happy birthday?"

"You did what I taught you. You don't kill at home, Laura. Not unless this isn't gonna be your home anymore. You thinking about moving?"

"No."

"What's there to talk about then?"

He knocked his glass into mine and drank his tequila down. Then almost as an afterthought, he kissed me. His hand moved slowly up my thigh, fingers flexed against then slipped under my thigh, tightening. He pulled me closer still. My free hand slid across his bare head, the other hand still held the glass of tequila. The burn from the previous shots seemed to spread faster, spiraling out from my spine and down each limb until every inch of me burned. Then he was gone, pulling away from me, standing and retreating to the doorway.

"I shouldn't have done that," he said.

I sat up straighter on the couch and tried to blink away the new light I saw him in. "Eight years and you've never even looked at me twice."

"Maybe you weren't paying attention." I opened my mouth but he put up a hand to stop me. "I promised Simon I wouldn't. Even when he let you go, he couldn't give you up. You'll always be his."

"He made you promise?"

"Guess he thought we were getting along too well."

"But you never liked me."

"You grew on me but I promised." Frank didn't break promises. Or give back money. His word was everything to him. If he said someone would be dead at three o'clock on Wednesday, it would happen. So he promised Simon.

I licked my lips. "So what was the kiss then?"

"Happy birthday," he shrugged. I couldn't read him. Eight years and I was only beginning to figure out Frank. I knew what kind of killer he was. But that was work and this was something else.

I fanned the flames in my system with another swallow of tequila and considered having another. "You could stay," I heard myself say. I crossed a line. I'd drunk too much. I may not have known Frank but he knew me. He walked over and pulled the glass from my hand, removed the bottle of birthday tequila from my sight and walked me to my bedroom. "You could stay," I said again.

"I can't. I have somewhere to be. Go to sleep." He lay me down on my bed and pressed his lips to my forehead. The slight spin to my world was nice and I wondered how much was because of the tequila and how much was because of Frank. I didn't hear him leave.

27

They never screwed around in Vegas. Simon would find out and Marjorie wasn't ready for that fight yet. And as long as he kept Laura working for him, she'd wanted to be able to tell him how wrong he was for it. So she only met Frank in places like this spa in Mesquite. Quiet and secluded, you paid your money and no one looked twice at you. Usually, she came for a day but sometimes she liked to stay here over the weekend, especially when she knew Simon would be out of town. Like this weekend. She'd driven up early, swam, had her massage and mani-pedi. Waxed and tanned, she felt invigorated. Or at least she had two hours ago, when Frank was supposed to get there. Now she was angry.

Simon had denied any physical relationship with her and yet Laura remained in his life. Marjorie had a hard time believing Laura was anything more than an office fuck he couldn't let go of. Which, of course, was the problem. Laura was younger than Marjorie, but not better looking. She was average at best and Marjorie was anything but. Her blonde hair was thick and healthy. Her body was strong and tight. Her legs, easily her best feature, were long and she was proud at her level of flexibility. Not that Simon cared to flex her the way she'd like. Marjorie still hadn't put together the aspects of Laura that made her so desirable to her husband. So desirable that her husband tried to hide his conversations with her. He always tried to make it business when he spoke to her in Marjorie's presence but he could never quite convince her that he was done with Laura.

Frank was another story. Their arrangement was new, they'd crossed paths in a club had a few drinks and then parted company. Marjorie had only wanted to be polite to her husband's employee. Of course, she knew what Frank did for Simon. It made him seem a little more dangerous and made his menacing looks seem more attractive. His hands, rough and callused, continent-sized hands. All that rough, so sweet and gentle in bed. Simon was good in bed too. He just didn't seem to be that interested in sleeping with her anymore.

Frank was waiting for her when she left the club that night, leaned up against her car. He claimed it was his job to make sure she got home in one piece. She laughed until she realized he was serious. Simon had Frank following her. She had been outraged. She focused that anger and irritation into one single thought. Revenge.

She kissed Frank. He didn't push her away. She went further, slipping her fingers behind his waistband and pulled out his shirt. Scraped her nails along his stomach. He backed her against the garage wall and kissed her deep, pressed her hard against his body and left her dazed. Then he helped her weak-kneed self into her car and followed her to the gates of her subdivision. He drove off without even a wave good-bye. Marjorie called him three days later from this very spa. He was there in two hours and she was well fucked an hour later.

Frank didn't talk much and getting him to talk about Laura was near impossible. He'd only say that she did what she was told and had never asked about Marjorie. Frank never answered more personal questions about himself or Laura. Marjorie suspected him of harboring feelings for Laura too. She'd never ask though. Not for the first time she wondered what it was about Laura that inspired such close-lipped loyalty from the men in her life.

There was a knock on her suite door. She smiled, flipped her hair over one shoulder and let Frank in.

"We need to talk," was all Frank said as he brushed past her. Marjorie gritted her teeth and forced a pleasant smile.

It was a dream that woke me. I yanked the sheet off and went to the bathroom. I ran the shower, picked a temperature between too hot and skin removal and threw myself into the cascade of water. Frank's face loomed large in my disquiet dreams. Simon, as always, was on the periphery. Close enough to see and smell, but always too far away to get a grip on. I'd woken up with the feeling that I had to do this. This was my chance. I could have Simon back. Me in his bed again, under his body again.

So many things could go wrong. Simon wouldn't set me up, I was sure of that. But would he protect me? That was always Frank's job. He was the one who saved me time and again. Simon sent me; Frank protected me.

Simon, Marjorie and Me.

I turned the water off, ran a towel across my body and forced still damp legs into my jeans. I threw on a shirt and headed out. It was only ten p.m. I could borrow a car and sit and wait, because sometimes Mrs. Pritchard left town. It couldn't hurt to get a feel for her days and nights.

The Pritchards lived in a gated community at the edge of the city. I was in a black Cadillac borrowed from a valet I knew. I gave him fifty and he slipped me the keys to one of the hotel's long-stay guest's car.

The difficulty was not in the waiting but in figuring out who was driving the black BMW that went past, two hours later. I knew it was Simon's car by the license plate, 'TAKE IT'. I waited until the car went through the intersection then I pulled out to follow. The car ahead of me drifted left then corrected, drifted right and corrected again. Had to be Marjorie. Simon could drive straighter than that with his eyes closed. I followed her through town as she guided the car down streets, avoiding the freeways. Twenty-five minutes later she pulled into the Fitzgerald's parking garage downtown. Simon would have disowned me if he'd seen me in the Fitzgerald's when we were dating. It was local and the real players of Las Vegas never went there. The Palms, Bellagio, even the travesty that was Bally's, would be a better place to be seen than the Fitzgerald's. Of course, now that we weren't a we anymore, I ate there pretty regularly with Frank. Frank liked it because no one bothered him. I liked it because I'd never run into Simon or the lovely Mrs. Pritchard there. Or so I thought.

Marjorie drove up and up. I figured she was headed for the top floor. I parked one floor down and took the stairs up to the last level. She'd parked and gotten out by the time I made it up there. She even had time to have herself plastered to the side of the car by a large man. The hand I could see gripped her narrow ass. I assumed the other hand was involved in the same maneuver. Marjorie's arms were around his neck and her head was tilted in my direction. The long blonde sheath of hair seemed to glow in the lights from the neon signage. I walked over and let the smile I felt tickling the edges of my mouth burst forth. My smile was on full wattage when the lovers ended their embrace. I think I stopped breathing when Frank's face turned toward me.

"You followed me," Marjorie said. I watched Frank pat her ass affectionately.

"Relax, Marjorie," he said. He stepped away from her, gently pulling her arms away from his neck and chest. She resisted and then relinquished him.

"Laura, what are you doing here?" His face was relaxed but the way he positioned himself between Marjorie and me told me he thought he already knew.

"I didn't come for her," I said, willing my voice to sound even.

"Good." He continued to close the distance between us.

"Would you have stopped me if I had?"

He ignored the question and kept coming closer. "It's good you're here. The three of us need to talk." When I was close enough he reached out and wrapped his hand around my wrist and pulled me a step to him. I looked up into those hard blue eyes and saw a flicker of regret there.

"So talk," I said, pulling away.

"We have an opportunity here," Frank said.

"How's that?"

"If we were to work together and remove him from the picture, there is a lot of money to be had."

"Him?" I looked from Frank's face to hers. She stood there with her hands on the wall as if at any moment she was ready to run at me. Frank walked between us and stood close enough I could feel the heat from his body again. I ran my tongue over my lips. The memory of the kiss was still fresh and easily accessible. He caught the movement, smiled a little.

"Laura, Simon is the problem," he said low, for my ears only. A breeze brought the faint smell of perfume to me. Her perfume was all around him. Stuck to him. Just like it was all over Simon. Every time I got near Simon I smelled this scent. A lingering, cloying, sweet scent.

"She's the problem. Can't you see that?"

"The money," Frank said.

"No." I turned to head back downstairs.

"He'll never let you go. You know that. He expects you to always be here. He'll find someone else. He'll always find someone else. Don't you see that?"

I turned back. From behind Frank, she stared me down and I realized then what Simon had in her. I may have been a killer but she was the truly dangerous one. All this time I had been static and Marjorie had always been in full motion, plotting and planning her next moves. Simon must have seen her for what she was finally. Frank was right. Simon wanted me. Who wouldn't? A woman who took his orders with a smile and yessir-may-I-have-another attitude. I looked Marjorie in the eye and said, "I'll do it."

"How do I know you won't come after me?" she said.

I walked over and yanked her hand off the wall. I uncurled those precious fingers of hers and stuck my hand inside her grip and I squeezed until her eyes widened and I thought she was good and scared. Then I let go.

"You don't know."

30

I agreed to help but that didn't mean I wanted to see Frank. I couldn't help but feel betrayed. Of course, the next night, Frank came to the house. He stood on my porch waiting to be let in. A gesture of sorts, usually he just walked in the second I opened the door but tonight he just stood there looking at me.

"You gonna ask me in?"

"What do you want?"

"Come on, Cupcake." He leaned in the doorway, a half-smile on his face.

"What? She doesn't need your services tonight?"

Frank sighed. "I'm sorry I didn't tell you."

"No, you're not. If I hadn't shown up last night you would have kept me in the dark as long as possible. That was a detail I didn't need to know. You figured she'd be a distraction, my dislike for her splitting my focus from your goal." He straightened and stepped into the hallway. I blocked him. "Why are you sleeping with her?"

"Something to do, I guess."

"But why her, of all people? Are you trying to hurt me?"

"How could I hurt you? You don't love me. She doesn't love me and Simon doesn't love anyone but himself, so who's getting hurt?" Frank said.

"He loved me."

"He left you for her."

"And now you're screwing her, which brings us back to my question: why her?"

"I'm not trying to hurt you. I'm sorry if have, okay?"

"Is this about him? Payback, revenge or is it you just marking territory?"

"Funny, but no. Wait, can I mark you?" He grinned down at me.

"Don't be cute now."

"Why are you so angry?"

"Because she sinks her claws into everything that's mine and claims it for herself. I thought she had money. I thought she had position. Why does she need you?" The sob that escaped surprised me. I took a deep breath. "Now she wants Simon gone."

"You don't?"

I sighed. "I just want out."

He lowered his face to mine. "What do you do when someone's blocking your way?" My teacher was back.

"I go through them," I said.

He ran his hand across my cheek, smearing the tears. "Good girl." He turned away. "You know, you stopped needing me a long time ago," he said as he stepped off my porch and onto the loose gravel of my driveway. "I always figured you'd stop needing him before now. But now will do." He got in his car and drove away.

31

Simon wanted to meet me for dinner. We met at The Mighty-Mighty. On a Wednesday night, the few patrons present cared little about what you were doing or whom you were doing it with. I dressed carefully for the occasion. The neckline of my red dress was respectable but the back was nonexistent. The skirt flared over my hips and ended just above my knee. My hair was swept back in a loose bun. It would look nice when he took it down. He loved to stroke my hair. I expected tonight to be no different. Black pumps, evening bag and no panties completed my ensemble.

He arrived ahead of me. He stood and took my coat, assessed me. "You look perfect." He breathed into my ear, warming my birthday diamonds.

"Thank you. So to what do I owe this evening?" I asked getting into the booth, gliding over the faux leather.

"I'm hoping you'll reconsider my request."

The waitress came over and he ordered for us. We waited for our drinks in silence but his hand managed to brush against mine. Our drinks arrived and I made a point of holding mine with two hands.

"If I do this for you, what does it mean?" I asked.

"What does it mean?"

"Yeah," I said, "what does it mean? Are we back together? Is it for real this time or just until you find another woman who looks the part you want her to play?"

"Laura," he said, scooting closer to me until we were side by side. "I made a mistake. I'm trying to correct that mistake." His fingers brushed my neck leaving behind trails of heat. My eyes closed. He shifted closer and kissed my neck.

"Simon," I whispered putting a hand on his chest. "The average husband divorces his wife."

"I'm not average." He sat back looking injured. He finished his drink and signaled the waitress with his uplifted glass. She nodded.

"No, you're not," I agreed, "but still."

"Do this for me." He was back kissing me and suddenly it was too hot. I broke our kiss and ran my hand down his chest and stomach then my hand slipped down his pants. That got him going. I was sure now, with every gasp, that his proper wife had never, would never, do the things I did for him. She could never turn him on like I did. His eyes were wide but left my face.

"You know I'd do you right here if you asked me too. Right here with everyone watching," I said, biting his earlobe.

"You're crazy," he managed.

"Crazy for you, only you." He turned his head to kiss me but I backed off him, my hand slithering out and away from him. The waitress returned with his drink. If she noticed Simon's altered state, breathing hard and sweating, she said nothing.

"I'll do it," I said, after she left.

"Good," he said his hand on my thigh inching upwards, "because I already transferred the money to you."

"Confident as usual."

His hand ascended another inch and now he knew what I wasn't wearing. He leaned into me again, his breath hot in my ear, "I'm always confident and you're the only person I trust. Now can we get out of here?" I nodded and we paid.

We got in his car and headed to the closest bed we could find. His hand on my leg was sending tingles through my body then he started to turn in at the Nocturne and my breath caught. The Nocturne with its staggered buildings, no security and an exit in the back was perfect place to kill a man. I knew Simon would come here. Frank and I had planned on it but here I was second-guessing. Around the corner, Frank would be waiting. The car's front tires hit the driveway. I could betray Frank or I could betray Simon.

I opened my mouth and, "Not here." fell out unbidden. Simon slowed the car and turned to me. I smiled brightly at him. "Remember when we stayed at Union?" He smiled at the memory, backed the car out into traffic and drove another quarter mile to the Union. Decision made; damage done.

Those were longest minutes I'd ever experienced. I looked in the side mirror searching traffic, looking for any car that appeared to be following us. Then at the Union, I had to grip the door handle when another car entered the parking lot to give me something to do other than scream. It wasn't anyone I knew and they didn't stop to look at the car or me. I stayed in the car while Simon checked in. We drove around to the back, found our room and didn't bother with the bed. He kissed my nerves away and, up against the motel's door, we time-traveled back to before his wedding, to a time before he broke my heart.

Spent, we collapsed onto the floor. He grinned at me. I moved off him and tried to smile back. He got up and walked to the bathroom pulling up his pants. I pulled my clothes back into position and peeked out the window. The parking lot looked empty. He came out smiling.

"Hey, baby." He cupped my face and kissed me again. His hands slipped down my neck to my shoulders. He pushed the dress off one shoulder and kissed it.

"I'm sorry," I said.

"For?" His hands sought out my dress's zipper. I stopped him.

"Marjorie wants you dead. Frank, too."

He stepped away from me. "What?"

"I told them I'd help them set you up. We're supposed to be at the Nocturne."

He flew at me. His hand around my throat, my feet barely touching the ground. I grabbed the arm that held me but I didn't fight him. He had me up against the window. The polyester curtain scratched my back. I hung there, the blood pounding in my head. He put his face in mine. "What have you done?"

"I'm sorry."

He pressed his body against me. He released my throat and pushed his face against my neck. I let my hands fall to my side.

"Why?" His voice reverberated against my neck. The sweet feel of his lips on my throat. He punched the wall next to my head. I jumped.

"It doesn't matter. You need to go." I said. My fingers gripped his lapels and I hung onto him for a second. Then I pushed him away.

He stared at me. "I'm done with you." He reached past me for the doorknob. As the door opened, he looked at me again. His mouth opened to say something more but all I heard was the gunshot. He staggered back into the room. His momentum made the door swing open. Marjorie was there, anger contorting her pretty face. She stepped into the room. Simon looked at me. He fell to his knees then over face down on the floor, with a soft grunt. He lay there bleeding. I crawled to him, whispering, "I'm so sorry." I turned him over.

"I knew we couldn't trust you. Frank said different but I knew."

I heard the door close. I pressed my hands into his hair and whispered I'm sorry again and again to him. Willing him to hear me, to understand.

Simon gave a little moan. I imagined his blood, soaking into the crappy carpet beneath him and straight through to the concrete then into the earth itself.

"Get away from him." Marjorie pushed me away with the muzzle of the gun. The hard edge digging into my ribs. Our eyes met and then I focused on the gun. It trembled in her hand but I knew she was serious. She was tired of me always in her way. I never thought about what it was like for her always knowing I was around her husband. Maybe she had loved him once. Maybe she had tried to be a good wife but there I was always trying to catch his eye. Always trying to get him back. I closed my eyes and waited for the follow-through. I heard the door open again and Frank's voice washed over me.

"Don't," he said.

"Told you she'd do this," Marjorie said.

"Put the gun down."

"No! She's the problem. Can't you see that?"

The echo of words I'd said to Frank snapped me out of my stupor. I stood. She raised the gun, her finger on the trigger.

"I'm leaving," I said.

"The hell you are," she said.

Again, Frank stood between us. He said, "Let her go."

"She can't be trusted. Look what she's done. She's ruined everything."

"No, she hasn't. It'll be fine."

I grabbed my purse off the floor and made my escape while they argued. I ran down the street, turned left and ran into a wedding party. The bride and groom all smiling faces, long-neck beer bottles in hand. Their friends crowded around them pushing me into the street. A cab went by but ignored me as I waved. I crossed the street and waved down another cab. Safe in the back seat I watched the wedding party weave their way down the street as we pulled away.

Twenty minutes later, I was home. I stood in the street watching the red lights disappear then I walked to my door. The gravel announced my every step and as I drew closer, I half-expected Simon to appear. I opened the door, prepared to see him on our couch, in our bedroom, but the house was full of quiet.

I packed a bag with some jeans, T-shirts, underwear and a sweater. I pulled a quilt from the closet and a pillow off the bed and loaded everything into the truck. I changed into jeans, tank top and sweatshirt, grabbed my backpack and headed into the backyard. I opened the little tool shed, dug up the six inches of dirt that covered a one-foot-by-three-feet long concrete slab, pulled on the corner to lift it out. In the space beneath almost fifteen thousand dollars sat in freezer bags. It should be enough to last me for a time. I could get more later if I needed it. I loaded the backpack, went back into the house and unplugged everything. The few thousand in my local bank account would cover the bills and the house—well, I guess I'd just have to let it go. I needed to let everything go now. Simon was dead.

Somewhere between Vegas and Santa Fe, Simon's body would be dumped. The hotel room cleaned and the witnesses paid off or buried. Frank wouldn't miss anything. Frank would be looking for me soon if he wasn't on his way already. Marjorie would insist. Or maybe she'd come after me herself. No, it would be Frank emerging from some dark corner of whatever new life I made for myself. No matter what he'd said I knew Frank would never just let me go. Frank didn't believe in loose ends.

THE END

About The Author

Nikki Dolson lives and writes in Las Vegas. Her stories have appeared in ThugLit, Day One, and Bartleby Snopes, among other places.

You can find her online at www.NikkiDolson.com

More books from Fahrenheit Press

If you enjoyed All Things Violent by Nikki Dolson you might also like these other Fahrenheit titles

Boondoggle By Mark Rapacz

Jukebox By Saira Viola

Sparkle Shot by Lina Chern

75506672R00100

Made in the USA
Columbia, SC
18 August 2017